Ulterior Motives

Other books by Laura Leone:

Romance Novels:
>One Sultry Summer
>A Wilder Name
>Ulterior Motives
>Guilty Secrets
>A Woman's Work
>Upon a Midnight Clear
>Celestial Bodies
>The Bandit King
>The Black Sheep
>Sleight of Hand
>Untouched by Man
>Under the Voodoo Moon
>Fever Dreams

Written as Laura Resnick:

Fantasy Novels:
>In Legend Born
>In Fire Forged

Non-Fiction
>A Blonde in Africa

Ulterior Motives

Laura Leone

WILDSIDE PRESS
Berkeley Heights, New Jersey

Ulterior Motives
A publication of
Wildside Press
P.O. Box 45
Gillette, NJ 07933-0045
www.wildsidepress.com

SECOND EDITION

For Mark and Lee Ann —
amis, amici, freunde, amigos —
friends in any language.

One

Shelley had noticed him instantly.

He had that certain something, that *je ne sais quoi,* that *savoir-faire.* He was the sort of man who stood out, even in a room as crowded as this one.

Shelley normally loathed the phrase "casual elegance," but it described this man too well to be cast aside. He looked so at ease in his tailored English suit and sleek Italian shoes that one would think he'd been born in them. He wore his gold cuff links and Swiss watch with notable unconcern. His straight, thick black hair was expertly cut in a continental style, and had been combed just carelessly enough to hint at an underlying sensuality. His blue eyes studied the crowd from beneath long dark lashes, his expression showing a subtle mixture of amusement and polite interest.

He looked very smooth and polished and clever. The best course of action, Shelley decided sensibly, would be to ignore him completely.

But she found, much to her surprise, that she kept noticing him. Within moments she noticed that he had noticed her, too, and was continuing to notice her. Soon, a little harmless noticing had turned into a staring contest.

His expression was flattering as he obviously absorbed the shock of her bold stare. Something electric passed between them in that crowded, noisy room, and the look on his face deepened to frank admiration and interest. Shelley didn't blush or turn away. She didn't understand the modern Western inhibitions regarding eye contact between strangers. If you found someone interesting, it seemed only polite to let your eyes tell them so; everyone needed a little positive reinforcement now and then. What's more, Shelley knew she could learn a lot about someone in those silent moments of eye contact. She had worked with the public all of her adult life and relied on her intuitive understanding of most people.

This was different, though. There was something fascinating about this man's lively blue eyes, something enigmatic about the smile hovering at the corners of his well-shaped mouth, something compelling about the way his relaxed body radiated dynamic energy.

He pushed himself lazily away from the pillar he'd been leaning against and started to walk purposefully toward her. Their gazes were still locked. Shelley felt transfixed. She had no idea what she would say once he reached her side. "Hello" seemed too banal, but "I can't stop staring at you" would sound ridiculous. The look in his eyes assured her that he would know exactly what to say. Shelley suddenly felt something monumental was about to happen to her.

"Watch out, there!" someone shouted.

It wasn't quite the extraordinary event she had been expecting. A waitress bumped into her and dropped three glasses of sangria all over Shelley's pale yellow blouse and gray wool skirt.

She gasped as the cold liquid drenched her chest and looked down in dismay at her besmirched outfit.

"Oh, no!" she said, for lack of something better to say.

"Oh, miss, I'm so sorry. Oh, excuse me, miss, no, here, let me do that. Oh, it's all my fault . . ." The overwrought waitress who had drenched her started brushing her off rather frantically.

"It's all right. Don't worry about it," Shelley replied placatingly as she dodged the girl's violent efforts to clean her stained blouse and skirt. "Really. I was standing right in your way."

"You certainly were," agreed Wayne Thompson. "Why were you standing there like a totem pole?"

Shelley gave her young, clean-cut colleague a sheepish look. "You'll have to stay here and talk to the client. I've got to go home and change. And for goodness' sake, try to be a little tactful."

Wayne looked around the large reception hall at the several hundred guests of Shelley's potential client, Keene International Company. New to Cincinnati, the company was throwing this big, rather expensive afternoon reception to celebrate its first year in the Queen City. They had invited all their current and potential business associates. Shelley, as the director of the Babel Language Center, was currently negotiating with Keene to handle all of their language and cultural training, as well as all of their translation and interpretation work. Although Keene clearly seemed to prefer Babel to Shelley's chief competitor, she wouldn't count her chickens until she had signed the contract with this important client. It would be a tremendous account for the language center and would likely lead to her promotion.

"How are you going to get home if I stay? Didn't you come by bus this morning?" Wayne prodded.

"Yes," she admitted distractedly. Unfortunately, at this time of day, the bus from downtown to her home on Mount Adams only ran once every hour. Furthermore, even if she felt like walking to the bus stop and waiting, she had left her coat at the Babel Language Center. It would take ten minutes to walk along the covered downtown skywalk to get back to the language center and grab her coat. Then she'd have to wait for the bus and finally sit through its circuitous route to Mount Adams. "I won't get back to work until nearly closing time," she said aloud in annoyance. The thought of paying for a taxi all the way home rankled her thrifty nature.

"There's really no need for me to stay," Wayne pointed out.

Shelley considered this for a moment. Wayne was the accountant at the language center, and talking with clients really wasn't part of his job.

"No," she said at last. "I want you to stay and keep an eye on that awful man. I don't trust him."

"Who?"

"Chuck."

Wayne raised his blond eyebrows. "Charles Winston-Clarke?"

"Yes." Shelley glanced about but didn't see her competitor, the director of the Elite Language Center. "If he's going to make one last-ditch effort to get a contract with Keene, he'll do it today. And I want to know about it."

"What makes you think they'd still be interested in Elite?"

"They invited Chuck to this party, didn't they?" Shelley argued in a low tone. "Anyhow, I saw him about ten minutes ago, and he looked even more nervous than usual. I want to know what he's up to."

"Maybe he just hates parties."

"Mmm," Shelley grunted noncommittally. There was something different about Chuck today. After all the underhanded, unprofessional, petty nonsense she'd had to put up with from her chief competitor, she had learned to keep a suspicious eye on him.

"Shelley, you're dripping all over this plush carpet," Wayne pointed out.

"And I'm freezing cold. I've got to get out of here," she said distractedly. Something was missing. Her stranger. Her handsome stranger. The man who had put her in a catatonic trance in the first place, so that some rookie waitress wound up spilling bright red sangria all over her. Feeling eyes upon her, Shelley looked up from her whispered conversation with Wayne.

He was still there. He looked suave, immaculate, and vastly amused. Shelley scowled at him. He grinned back, and his smile was breathtaking. It was genuine and warm and disarmingly sexy, and it lit up his whole face. She stared at him while he walked to her side.

"I'll take you home," he said simply.

Shelley kept looking at him while Wayne asked the obvious question:

"Who are you?"

"I'm a friend of . . ." He raised one gleaming black brow inquisitively as he paused.

"Shelley," she supplied.

"Shelley," he repeated softly, as if she had answered a very important question.

Wayne looked speculatively at Shelley. Shelley looked at her handsome stranger with some misgivings. Instinct told her he was the most fascinating man she'd ever seen. Common sense told her he could be a kidnapper, a white slaver or even, God forbid, a sports fanatic. It would be very foolish to get into a car alone with him. However, she might never see him again, and she didn't want to let this moment slip by. After all, how often did life resemble a Frank Sinatra song?

"Well, perhaps . . ."

At that moment hordes of apologetic waiters, doormen, managers and businessmen descended on Shelley, who was still standing around in a very wet, very dirty blouse, courtesy of their newest waitress. All the attention was a bit overwhelming. After assuring them that she would indeed bill them for the damage and insisting they give the befuddled waitress another chance before firing her, Shelley was more than willing to cooperate with her handsome stranger when he took her hand in his and led her away from the brouhaha.

They left the hotel's reception room, rode the escalator to the ground floor, and walked through the plush lobby to the Fountain Square exit.

"Jacket?" he inquired before they left the building.

"No, I came on the skywalk."

He opened the door for her, and they stepped outside. The April air was pleasant, but it was still too cold to be outside in only a blouse, and a wet one at that. She hoped he hadn't parked far away. He noticed her shiver.

"Why don't you go back inside and wait?" he suggested. "My car is parked in the garage under Fountain Square. I won't be more than a minute."

She agreed readily. She was cold and now she'd have one last chance to decide whether she was really going to get into a car with a total stranger who'd picked her up at a party, albeit a very respectable party.

He gave her an amused look just before he walked off, as if he knew exactly what she was thinking — and as if he knew she'd go with him, anyway.

He walked the way he spoke: confidently, smoothly. She'd noticed not so much an accent in his voice as a complete lack of one. As someone who had studied languages and linguistics for years, she tended to be instantly aware of such things. He spoke with what she considered a mid-Atlantic voice, neither American nor English, but somewhere in between. Often people who had been raised in two or more countries spoke that way, because they'd lacked a consistent colloquial speech model.

He disappeared into the underground garage, and she felt his absence instantly. Curiously enough, she didn't suddenly come to her senses and decide to call a taxi. She had never before been attracted to anyone at first glance like this, and she wanted to know what it was about him that fascinated her so. Was it simply his impressive façade? Was she a pushover for dark good looks, sparkling blue eyes, and a well-cut suit over a well-developed body? Had she fallen for the old smoldering-gaze-across-the-room technique?

Somehow she doubted it. She might not have a good head for math and she might not have a natural fashion sense, but she was perceptive about people. From the moment she'd laid eyes on him, she had sensed an extraordinary man under that admittedly spectacular exterior.

And it seemed the only way she'd find out more was to let him drive her home to change her clothes.

True to his word, he pulled up momentarily outside the hotel. Upon seeing the car, Shelley probably would have gotten in even if he had been Jack the Ripper.

It was a red Porsche convertible.

She had wanted to ride in a red Porsche convertible her whole life. She *belonged* in one. She saw herself driving it along some curvy mountain road in the sunset, expertly negotiating the hairpin bends of the treacherous surface, like Emma Peel, like one of Charlie's Angels, like the Girl from U.N.C.L.E. . . .

In any event she certainly couldn't refuse her first chance to ride in one.

He got out of the car and came around to open the door for her, a rather pleasing and old-fashioned courtesy she had forgotten about.

"I don't suppose we could let the top down?" she asked after he slid gracefully into the driver's seat.

He smiled at her again. The effect really was quite devastating, like being hit in the solar plexus. The sheer sexuality of it took her breath away. And his teeth were so white that his mother must be awfully proud.

"It's just that I've always wanted to ride in one of these with the top down"

"Yes, I can tell," he said dryly.

"And I'm afraid this will be my only chance."

He studied her enthused expression for a moment before saying simply, "I don't think this will be the last time, do you, Shelley?"

At a loss for a neutral answer, she instead asked a question. "What's your name?"

He nodded, as if glad she'd finally remembered to ask. "Ross. Ross

Tanner." He pulled away from the curb, entered the stream of traffic, and asked, "Where do you live?"

"Mount Adams. Do you know how to get there?"

"Haven't the faintest."

"Turn right up here. Why did you offer to drive me home?"

"Because I didn't want you to leave without me. Now what?"

"Go to the bottom of the hill. Why not?"

He risked a brief glance at her, then turned his attention back to the traffic. His look had been challenging. "Why were you staring at me? Do I turn at the light?"

"No, the second light."

"Which way?" he asked.

"Left."

"You haven't answered my question."

"I'm not sure. Why were you staring at me?"

"Because you're a beautiful woman who was staring at me."

That left Shelley at a loss for words. He was right. She had started it, but she didn't think of herself as beautiful. Terminally cute, perhaps, and that was a look she did her best to minimize so she would be taken seriously at work. She was five feet two inches, with high, full cheeks and big, round gray eyes. Her shoulder-length coppery hair was deplorably frizzy. She had tried cutting it once, but the effect was too chipmunklike to be borne; now she usually wore it in a high ponytail, since it gave some illusion of being tall. She came dangerously close to being pleasingly plump, and now that she had an office job, only infrequent and frantic exercise kept her tummy flat and her curves in place.

She had finally left her adolescent insecurities about her looks behind and could accept that a number of men found her attractive. But "beautiful" was going too far. Did he need glasses or was he making a casual pass?

"Bear right," she said, suddenly aware he was about to go the wrong way. "You're not from around here, are you?"

"No, I've only just arrived," he admitted.

"Do you work for Keene International?"

"No. I may do business with them eventually, that's all."

"I see. Oh, it gets a little complicated here," she cautioned. She spent the next few minutes guiding him through the circuitous route to the slope of Mount Adams.

"In all of Cincinnati, you couldn't find a place easier to get to?" he asked.

"It's worth the effort," she assured him. "Turn right. This is the beginning of the neighborhood."

They drove slowly up the steep, narrow street, passing tall, turn-of-the-century town houses with long staircases descending the sloping hills to the road. Most of the buildings were newly renovated, and their ornate ironwork, careful craftsmanship, and solid carpentry were complemented by spanking new paint and well-tended yards. In addition to homes, the area was teeming with coffee shops, wine bars, antique shops, florists, jewelry makers, and unusual small businesses.

"But unfortunately there's no grocery store," Shelley explained as they drove along. "And it's very hard to get up and down here on bad winter days."

"I can imagine. Still, it's a beautiful area."

"Stop here. I live in there." She pointed to a tall yellow townhouse with a large verandah on the first floor and a small balcony overlooking the Ohio River Valley. "The apartment on the second floor. I pay more for the balcony, but I just saw myself on that balcony, you know?"

"Yes, I see you there, too."

She looked at him. Charismatic or not, he was a total stranger, and there was no way she was letting him into her apartment while she changed her clothes. She had seen too many TV shows where women who did things like that disappeared forever.

He seemed to sense her anxiety, and for the first time that day, the amusement faded from his eyes. His expression grew suddenly soft and serious, and she saw then just how strong his face was, how much character resided there.

"Listen, Shelley, I know your mother told you not to accept rides from strange men, and she was absolutely right."

"That's *exactly* what my mother said. How did you know that?"

"Everyone's mother says it. Mine said it, too. But I was just standing around at this party full of nervous people all trying to have a good time, anxious businessmen trying to impress each other and harried waiters trying to make everyone comfortable. Then I looked up and saw you. You seemed beautiful and interesting and very smart, and you were looking at me as if you thought I might be all of those things, too. And you never turned away, which made you seem more interesting, because most people are so afraid to be caught staring at someone." He glanced away for a moment, as if gauging his next words carefully. "I wanted to talk to you. I still do. When it became obvious you'd have to leave, I was unwilling to let the opportunity slip by."

His deep blue eyes met her gray ones, and she felt herself sinking into their depths. He had stated his case plainly and wanted to know where she stood. What was it about this man that made her feel she knew him, when, in fact, she didn't know him at all? The thought of getting to know him excited and intrigued her.

"I'm going to go upstairs to change, and then you can drive me back to work. Maybe you'd like to have a cup of coffee with me in my office?"

"I'll be waiting right here," he said softly.

Something about his smooth voice, vibrating deep in his chest, went straight through her. She could listen to him talk all day. She could stare into those clear eyes fringed by thick black lashes till the cows came home. She could run her fingers through that gleaming black hair . . . Shelley took a deep breath and got out of the car.

She let herself into her one-bedroom apartment, a small, friendly place that had high ceilings, wooden floors, and big windows. It was haphazardly furnished with things she'd either bought on sale or managed to get secondhand from her mother before any of her siblings claimed them. The rooms were cheerfully cluttered with favorite souvenirs from her many trips in Europe, as well as with photographs of friends overseas and her family in Chicago.

She took off her clothes and looked at them critically. She would ask the dry cleaner what could be done, but she had a feeling they were history. She was impressed, actually, that Ross could speak so seriously to a woman with such huge red stains all over her clothes.

Shelley smiled when she thought of Ross and glanced out the window. He had gotten out of the car and was leaning against it while he surveyed the river valley below. He looked like a model in one of those terribly manly TV commercials for foreign sports cars.

She opened her closet and wondered what to wear. She had accepted some years ago that she didn't have a natural eye for what would look flattering on her. She had learned to settle for a working wardrobe of extremely simple clothes in easy-to-match colors paired with high-heeled shoes that could give her added height.

She didn't particularly regret the damage to her gray wool skirt. It was too long, and she had always had the feeling it made her look like she was standing in a hole. She wished, however, that she could think of some color combination or clever mixture of accessories that would knock Ross's socks off. He was definitely worth the effort.

After taking more time than she had meant to, she decided simplicity was still her best option. She donned a white blouse and straight black skirt. She realized belatedly, as she descended the front steps, that she probably looked like she should be serving food at a wedding reception.

Ross, however, wore a flattering expression as he opened the passenger door.

Shelley looked somewhat wistfully at the roof of his car as he started the engine.

"We'll put the top down next time," he promised. "Tomorrow's Saturday. Are you busy?"

"Well, I . . . There's a . . . I should . . . Nothing I can't cancel," she said finally. She had a list of errands as long as her arm, but that seemed very unimportant at the moment.

"Perhaps you could show me around a bit tomorrow?"

"I'd love to," she admitted. Then she grinned at him. "But only if you put the top down,"

"I promise."

"And I get to drive," she added.

He looked at her suspiciously, a slight smile hovering at the edges of his mouth. "We'll talk about it."

"Turn right at the bottom of the street and follow the signs for downtown."

"How do you usually get to work?"

"I bring my car if I know I'll be working late, but otherwise I take the bus. During rush hour it's a quick ride and it's much more convenient than fighting for a parking space."

She chatted comfortably with him the rest of the way downtown. They talked about various places they might go the following day, Shelley's passion for Chinese food, the local brands of Cincinnati beer Ross would have to try, how wonderful it was to see spring coming at last and whether or not fish still lived in the Ohio River.

He told her his favorite restaurant in the whole world was a little family-owned place in Toulouse, France. Shelley had been there, too, on one of her many trips through Toulouse. They laughed together as they remembered the big white dog that came around to inspect the leavings at every table. Ross was a pleasure to talk to, intelligent, charming, funny, his deep voice flowing through her with its smooth, round tones.

"If you turn down this street, there's usually a parking space free this late in the day. We're right by my office," Shelley said.

"Have you ever stopped to consider," he said absently as he backed the Porsche into the curbside space, "that parallel parking is really a rite of passage for modern man? Separates the men from the boys, as it were. I mean, would you still respect me if we got this far and I told you I couldn't park the car?"

"Well, I couldn't criticize, since parallel parking isn't my strong suit, and you might eventually find out."

"Very sensible. Shall we?" They got out of the car and started walking up the street. "I hope you make a good cup of coffee."

"My coffee's only so-so. But my secretary makes great coffee."

"Ah, you have a secretary. Are you some sort of important, top-level executive?" he asked as he offered her his arm.

"Hardly," she said, taking his arm and walking close beside him. He was tall, about six feet, she guessed, and she had trouble keeping up with his considerably longer legs. He slowed his pace instantly to one she could easily match. His arm felt strong and sturdy beneath his expensive suit, and she felt good walking with him, touching him.

"What do you do, then?"

"Over here," she said, pulling him toward an open-air escalator. "It's up on the skywalk. I'm the director of the Babel Language Center."

He pulled slightly away from her, surprise evident in his expression. "Babel?" he repeated in astonishment.

"I guess the name isn't exactly loaded with credibility," Shelley admitted. "But they're successful enough that I doubt if they'll change it. Anyhow it's actually quite a good language school."

"You know, Shelley," he said slowly, "I don't even know your last name."

"I hadn't even thought of that. It's Baird."

"Shelley Baird. Or Michelle Baird —"

"That's right."

"Director of the Babel Language Center."

"It's right over here." They turned right at the top of the escalator and walked past a boutique, a coffee shop, and two small businesses before coming to a big picture window and a glass door with the Babel logo printed on it. Shelley pushed open the door and led Ross into the lobby. It was tasteful but lacked elegance. It had been last decorated many years before Shelley's arrival, and she was still trying to convince headquarters to allot her some money to update it. In the meantime she did what she could to add some character to the place by adding plants and hanging prints.

"*Ciao,* Shelley," the receptionist greeted her. *"Ma come mai hai cambiato vestiti?"*

"*Ciao,* Francesca. There was a little accident at the reception, that's all."

The Italian woman's soft brown gaze rested on Ross with interest. Shelley was pleased to see she wasn't the only woman who couldn't help staring at him. Francesca, however, was happily married. Her interest was limited to subtle appreciation of some very masculine appeal.

"Francesca, this is Ross Tanner, who may or may not be connected to Keene International. Ross, this is our very capable secretary, Francesca Mannino."

"Molto piacere, signora," Ross said politely, taking Francesca's hand.

"Lei parla italiano, signore?" Francesca asked.

"Actually, no, I don't speak Italian, but a friend once taught me a dozen useful phrases for meeting Italian women."

"Such as?" Shelley asked with interest.

"Non ci conosciamo?" he said suggestively.

"'Haven't we met before?'" Shelley repeated. "That's a little shopworn, isn't it?"

"I said they were useful, not original. Besides, I was young enough at the time to think that was a subtle approach." He grinned at her skeptical expression.

Shelley turned back to Francesca. "Any messages?"

"Yes, yes, many messages. Always it is the same when she leaves," Francesca confided to Ross. "The phone never stops ringing. Teachers want to talk to Shelley, clients want to talk to Miss Baird, she must call her superiors before five o'clock, or the world will come to an end. I think it is very irritating."

"Who called today?" Shelley asked patiently.

Francesca spoke to her for several minutes in mingled English and Italian, handing her note after note, explaining that a Spanish teacher was having trouble with the immigration authorities and needed Shelley to speak to them on his behalf, the interpretations coordinator needed Shelley to find a local Pashto speaker for a court case and the French teacher wanted to know whether someone else could teach the group class tonight because she was having rice.

"Rice?" Shelley repeated, frowning. "Are you sure she said rice?"

"I don't know what she said. She was crying."

"I think that must be 'crisis,' Francesca. I'd better sort that out right away. I can't have seven people show up at six o'clock to find there's no teacher and no lesson."

"Shelley, you've obviously got a lot to do," Ross said, "Perhaps it would be best if I left."

She looked at him regretfully, sorry to see him go, but she really did have too much to do this afternoon to spend any more time on personal matters. Anyhow she would be seeing him tomorrow. "Yes, maybe you're right. But at least let me show you around the school before you go."

He seemed torn for a minute, as if he were suddenly anxious to leave. After a brief moment he evidently made up his mind, since he politely said, "Yes, I'd love to see the rest of the school."

She showed him the teachers' lounge, Wayne's office, her own office, and the school's ten classrooms, ranging in size from small rooms for private lessons to a large room for group courses. Toward the back of the school was a coffee room where students and staff could congregate before lessons or during their breaks.

"There's another door back here that leads out to the street," Shelley said.

"I'll see you tomorrow then?"

"Yes."

"What time shall I pick you up?"

"How about ten o'clock?"

"All right." His gaze roamed her features, and he seemed as if he wanted to say more.

Always one for the direct approach, Shelley asked, "Is there something else?"

She could tell that whatever it was, he had changed his mind. Instead he looked at her with a very sensual expression in his eyes. He let his gaze drop to her mouth, and Shelley felt her face grow warm. He pulled her toward him and lowered his head very slowly, giving her time to pull away, as if she could possibly want to.

"Just this." He breathed against her lips an instant before his mouth touched hers in a soft kiss. It was a feather-light caress, warm and tender, lasting scarcely a second. They stayed with their faces close together, enjoying each other's nearness for a long, silent moment as they savored the promise in that brief kiss.

Shelley was amazed that a mere kiss could make her quiver, could suddenly fill her mind with erotic thoughts, could make her long to melt against him and find out what else he did so well.

"I could stay like this all day," he said softly. "But I only put a quarter in the parking meter."

Shelley smiled. "I'll see you tomorrow."

"Until tomorrow," he said, and left.

Shelley looked at the door after he'd gone, allowing herself one last moment of pleasure over him. Then she sighed and headed toward her office. Francesca stood in her doorway and peered at her curiously.

"You were back there a long time," Francesca said suggestively.

"Oh?" Shelley responded noncommittally.

"He is a real man," Francesca said enthusiastically.

"I suppose so," Shelley agreed, remaining nonchalant.

"You have found a good lover," Francesca said with great certainty.

"He's not my lover. He just gave me a lift," Shelley said casually.

"Ah, no, *cara*, he looks at you the way a real man looks at a woman he wants," Francesca declared with obvious relish.

"Have you nothing else to do today except *chiacchierare?*" Shelley prodded, feeling embarrassed at last.

"Ahh," Francesca said wisely, and went back to her desk.

Shelley was picking up the phone, hoping to secure a French teacher for that evening's class, when Wayne Thompson came bounding through the front entrance and charged into her office. He flung his lanky frame into a chair before her desk and shook his blond hair.

"Whatever you're doing, put it aside, put down the phone —" he snatched the receiver out of her hand "— and listen to me!"

"Yes, Wayne, has something happened?" Shelley asked dryly.

"You were right, I was wrong —"

"Heavens to Betsy."

"Mr. Charles Winston-Clarke has good cause to be uptight today."

"If this is about Chuck," Shelley interrupted, "it can wait till later."

"No, it can't. Wait till you get a load of this!" Wayne was just pushy enough to extract information from people that they really hadn't intended to give him, and Shelley was curious to know what had prompted his whirlwind entrance.

"Well?" she prodded.

"Well, since you came to Cincinnati over a year ago, we've given Elite very serious competition for new business. I might add that my own contribution to our success and their lack of it has not been negligible —"

"Get to the point."

"Patience, I am. It seems that while Cincinnati was a quiet little city with two quiet little unsuccessful language schools downtown, the folks at Elite's headquarters in Paris didn't pay any attention to either of us. But now the city is growing by leaps and bounds, and Keene International is just one of a number of big companies offering considerable opportunities to a reputable language center. The great minds at Elite are feeling somewhat perturbed that, while they've been concentrating their energies elsewhere, we've elbowed them out of all new business here this year."

"Well, that's their tough luck for not looking ahead," Shelley said flatly.

"Their thoughts exactly."

Shelley looked at him speculatively. "Are they thinking about replacing Chuck?"

"It's a little more interesting than that. They're sending a fix-it man."

"A what?"

"They've evidently got some guy whose whole job is to go around reorganizing schools that are losing money. He's directly responsible to Henri Montpazier, the president of the whole company, and to no one else."

"Is he some kind of marketing expert?" Shelley asked.

"I don't know what his actual background is. I'll have to ask around and find out more about him."

"How does he 'reorganize'?"

"Top to bottom. He comes in, figures out everything that's wrong with the center, finds a whole new staff if necessary, examines their finances, their methods, their location. He contacts new clients, old clients and *other schools'* clients, Shelley."

Shelley leaned back in her chair as she considered Wayne's words. "So they're not just bringing in someone to clean up their own act. They want a piece of our action, too."

Wayne nodded. "And we've always agreed that, even with all this new business coming into the city, there still aren't enough clients for our particular sort of business to keep two language centers in healthy operation."

"How good is this guy's reputation?" Shelley asked.

"Very good. From what I understand, he totally turned around their school in Washington last year. That didn't particularly hurt business at the Babel school there, but that's a much busier city than this one. I gather he reorganized an Elite school in some French city a few years back — Toulouse, I think Charles said it was — and the competing language center closed down."

"All right," Shelley said. "It looks like we may have a problem on our hands. I'll call Chicago to let them know what's happening and to see if we can find out more about this guy and his methods."

"I have a friend who used to work for Elite in New York. I'll call her and see what she can find out —"

Shelley hesitated for a moment, not liking the cloak-and-dagger quality of that. "All right," she said at last. "Go ahead. The more we know about what to expect, the better. And in the meantime let's keep in mind that this could all be hot air. I've never known Chuck to tell the truth before."

"I think he was telling the truth, Shelley. He seemed worried. If they decide they're not pleased with the way he's been running things, he'll be lucky to find himself running a one-room Elite outpost in northern Alaska by the time this is over."

"I'm still skeptical. I wish I'd been there to talk to Chuck myself," Shelley muttered.

"So do I. Did you have a nice chat with tall-dark-and-handsome, by the way?" Wayne asked slyly.

"Never mind that," Shelley chided. "You get on the phone and see if you can find a French teacher for tonight while I call Chicago." She picked up the phone and started dialing the long-distance number. "When is this guy expected to arrive?"

"He's already here. He arrived yesterday."

"He's here?" Shelley exclaimed. "Have you seen him?"

"No. I asked Charles to point him out at the reception, but he had disappeared." Wayne got up to leave.

"I'd have loved to have talked to him, too. Tell Francesca to hold my calls for the next . . . Wait!"

Drifting thoughts started to come together in Shelley's mind. Something about Toulouse and a man who had disappeared from Keene International's reception today . . . *I may do business with them eventually, that's all . . . Michelle Baird . . . Director of the Babel Language Center . . .*

With an oppressive sense of irony she asked Wayne suddenly, "Did you find out what his name is?"

"Ross Tanner."

Shelley slammed the phone down just as it started ringing in Chicago. "Somehow I thought you'd say that," she said, and rubbed her fingers against her temples as if she had developed a sudden headache.

"What's wrong?"

"Sit down. I have something to tell you."

Two

"Let me get this straight," Wayne said incredulously. "You not only invited Ross Tanner up here, you actually showed him around?"

Shelley nodded. "Francesca!" she called. "Have you got anything for a headache?"

"Well, gee, Shelley," Wayne continued facetiously, "as long as he was here, why didn't you show him our books, tell him about our latest contracts, and let him sit in on a few language lessons?"

"Stop it! I had no idea who he was. The only thing he said about his line of work was that he might do some business with Keene International. I didn't know he was connected to Elite. How could I have known?"

"All right, all right, I'm sorry. The damage is done —"

"No damage was done! All he did was look around a bit. For goodness' sake, even Chuck has been here before!"

"Why did you bring Tanner here in the first place? Was it his idea?"

"No . . ."

"You suggested it?"

"Yes . . ."

"Why, for God's sake?"

"Because he took me home and then drove me back to work. I invited him up here for a cup of coffee. I was just trying to be polite." That wasn't the whole truth, but Shelley was determined to keep certain mistakes private.

"All right, even assuming that he really didn't know who you were, why didn't he say something once he realized his mistake?" Wayne challenged.

"That's what I'd like to know," Shelley muttered.

"He was thinking about other things, maybe," suggested Francesca knowingly as she entered the room with a bottle of aspirin and a glass of water.

"What things?" pounced Wayne.

"That's enough, Francesca," said Shelley. "Give me that. My head is killing me."

"What things?" Wayne repeated. "Francesca, did he seem unusually interested in something up here?"

"Yes, he was very interested —"

"Francesca," Shelley warned.

"In Shelley."

Both Wayne and Francesca turned to stare at Shelley speculatively. Francesca looked at her with fond concern, while Wayne seemed convinced his boss had lost all her marbles.

"And you fell for that?" he demanded.

"I didn't fall for anything!" Shelley insisted hotly.

"My God, Shelley, of all the men to pick —"

"That's enough, Wayne! I made a mistake, that's all. He caught me off my guard, but it won't happen again. He didn't see or hear anything up here that's going to suddenly lead to our dramatic downfall. Now I think we all have too much work to do to waste any more time dwelling on why he didn't tell me the truth. He's obviously a very slippery character, that's all."

There was a moment of silence as they digested this. "All right," Wayne said at last, "you're right. We shouldn't overreact to this. I'll get on the phone and find someone for tonight's French class. You'd better call Chicago."

Shelley called her superior in Chicago to explain what they'd just learned. She decided not to tell him about the afternoon's events, since it was irrelevant and made her feel ridiculous.

"Have you ever heard of this guy, Jerome?" Shelley said into the receiver.

"No, but then he's obviously never come to the Midwest before. I'm supposed to call the New York office tonight and the Paris office on Monday morning. I'll ask about him then. If he's well known, they'll be able to provide information on him. In the meantime, Shelley, just don't let him come between you and that contract with Keene International. We're counting on you."

"Yes, Jerome."

"Call me around ten o'clock Monday morning with this week's figures, and I'll let you know what I've heard."

"Okay."

"Don't worry about it, Shelley. You're doing a great job. You've always made me glad that I recommended you for that post."

Shelley smiled. "Thanks, Jerome. I'll talk to you Monday."

Shelley worked late that night. This had nothing to do with Ross

Tanner or her worries about what kind of trouble he could cause. Shelley had increased business by more than thirty percent in the time she'd been director of the Babel school, but she still hadn't been supplied with the staff necessary to cope with that extra workload. She had requested an associate director and another secretary; headquarters in New York had denied these requests but promised to review the situation again the following year. So Shelley worked longer hours as business continued to grow.

Upon reflection she could perhaps believe Ross hadn't known who she was. He had seemed genuinely surprised when she told him she was the director of the Babel Language Center. At the time she had attributed his surprise to the rather unusual name of her business. It evoked images of the biblical Tower of Babel, the lust for power that had inspired its construction and the confusion that had followed its destruction by the Almighty. Shelley wished once again that the board of directors would choose a new name.

She went home feeling weary and distinctly hurt. Ross had seemed like the most wonderful man she'd ever met. Why hadn't he told her the truth before he left? Had he really had hopes of learning something significant from her before she found out who he was? Had he been playing with her? Was he embarrassed? She had sensed some indecision in him, and she still wasn't sure what to attribute it to.

Now that she knew who he was, she certainly couldn't see him again. Babel company policy prohibited teachers and staff from dating clients and students. Although Shelley disapproved of a business policy that tried to regulate employees' personal lives, she had abided by it during her sojourn in Cincinnati and had turned down several clearly personal invitations from male clients. Given that, she could hardly go out with her company's chief competitor, particularly not when he represented such a potential threat to the growth of her business.

At home she stuck some leftover Chinese food in the microwave and wondered whether Ross Tanner really could convince Keene International to go with Elite instead of Babel. She had another meeting scheduled with Keene on Tuesday. She would try to get a commitment from them then, before Ross had time to put together a new proposal.

There was not, as Wayne had pointed out, enough business to keep two language schools very busy. Competition for each new client was fierce. Shelley prided herself on her previously unsuspected talent for running a business and drawing new clients. However, she knew that she owed part of her rather impressive first-year success to the mediocrity of her competitor at Elite. Chuck was as incompetent as Shelley's predecessor, and probably a lot more dishonest — he was just better at hiding it. Shelley was still new enough to lack confidence in her ability to stay on top now that Elite had brought in an expert.

Ross would be coming to pick her up in the morning, she realized. She must decide now how to deal with him. She wanted to handle the situation with dignity, both for her self-respect and because, curiously enough, she wanted his respect, too. She decided she would be cool, businesslike, and firm, no matter what.

When Shelley opened her front door the next morning, Ross took one look at the total absence of warmth or welcome in her eyes and realized she already knew the truth.

"News travels fast around here, I see," he commented after a heavy silence.

"Especially bad news," Shelley said coolly.

"Can we talk about this?" he asked hopefully.

"I think I already know what I need to know."

"Shelley, I'm sorry. I didn't want you to hear it from someone else."

"Then you should have told me yourself yesterday," she said reasonably.

"Yes, I should have," he said with a sigh. "I just thought we would need some time alone to discuss our options, and there didn't seem much chance of talking to you alone in your office."

"Our options?"

"Can I come inside?"

"I think it would be better if you left now, Ross."

"I think it would be a big mistake to leave now," he countered as he leaned against the doorframe.

"Look, Ross, yesterday was very nice, but —"

"Nice?" he repeated. "Nice? Shelley, how often do you suppose something like yesterday happens to two people?"

"It happens all the time in Frank Sinatra songs."

"Well, yes," he said, slightly amused, "but how often has it happened to you?"

"That depends on which part of yesterday you're talking about. The part where you entered my office as a guest and neglected to tell me who you really were? The part where I felt like a fool after I found out? The part where I wondered why you hadn't been honest with me? The part where —"

He took her chin in his hand and forced her face up. His blue eyes were intense and his voice was low when he said, "I'm talking about the instant attraction between us and then very real pleasure we took in each other's company yesterday."

His touch was electric. His eyes were compelling. His voice burned straight through her, setting off little reactions deep in her belly.

"You deliberately misled me," she said shakily. "You're going to try to undermine my business. Why on earth should I trust you?"

"I'm not asking you to trust me, not yet, anyhow. Just to talk to me."

He didn't plead or cajole; he simply asked, and the effect was devastating on Shelley's system. She forgot what very sensible thing she had planned to say next.

"I . . . Um . . . You . . ."

"Let me in so we can talk about this," he whispered, his eyes holding hers.

He smelled so good, she thought irrelevantly, not of cologne or soap, just a clean, musky, male smell. Wordlessly she backed into the apartment while he followed her. He closed the door softly behind them and looked around the room. It suddenly seemed very intimate to have him here, and she hoped he would like it.

"It's like you," he said simply, obviously meaning it as a compliment. "Is that coffee I smell?"

Shelley nodded. "Would you like some?"

"I'd love some. I take it black."

She brought him a big colorful mug filled to the brim. His eyes were soft as he took it from her hands. He looked even better today than he had yesterday, casually dressed in tight blue jeans, a pale shirt, and a black leather jacket. His jet-black hair was windblown.

"You left the top down," she said suddenly.

"I promised, didn't I?" he teased. "We'll be lucky if we don't catch pneumonia, though."

Shelley looked wistfully out the window. "I'm tempted, Ross, but I just don't think we should pursue this any further. It just wouldn't be intelligent, or even responsible."

"Shelley," he said firmly, "I didn't know who you were until you told me. And I'm not interested in you in the hope that you'll let your guard down and say something I can use against you."

He looked so honest and strong. But he had looked that way yesterday, too. Maybe it was just a gift of bone structure.

"Shelley . . ." he prodded.

He was irresistible, which made her seriously question her judgment in this case. She wanted to be with him enough to talk herself into anything. That was also stupid and irresponsible.

"Not today," she said at last. "I have to think about this."

He saw the sudden determination in her eyes and realized that right now that was the best answer he would get. At least she hadn't told him never to darken her door again.

He let out his breath in a rush and put his coffee cup down in a graceful motion. Everything he did looked good, Shelley thought distractedly. It wasn't fair. He crossed the room swiftly. Before she knew what was happening, she was in his arms.

Ross lost himself in her eyes, which were warm and soft with confusion. "If you want time, you've got it. But I'll be thinking of you," he said huskily as he lowered his mouth to hers.

It wasn't the tender caress of yesterday; it wasn't an affectionate embrace; it wasn't a respectable ten-o'clock-in-the-morning kiss. His kiss was hot, passionate, and erotic. His tongue tickled her lips, then plunged without warning into her mouth to stroke and taste and explore. He shifted her against him quite suddenly so that their hips pressed close together while his mouth continued to pillage hers. His hands came down and stroked her bottom with a slow, firm caress that pulled her even closer. All Shelley saw was swirling black; all she heard was the sound of their mingled breath; all she felt was the hot pleasure of his touch, his kiss, his strong body against hers; all she thought was, *sweet, sweet, oh, that's so good.*

They were both breathing quickly when he released her. Finally Shelley remembered to open her eyes, and she was pleased to see that he looked almost as dazed as she felt.

"You're . . . awfully good at that," she admitted weakly.

"You inspire me," he whispered, and dropped a soft kiss on her forehead. He moved away from her and went to the front door. He paused on his way out. "I'll call you tomorrow."

"Not tomorrow," she protested breathlessly, wanting to beg him to stay.

"Monday, then."

"No . . . later."

"I'll call you," he repeated. He took one last look, his eyes seeming to burn through her clothes, then left, closing the door softly behind him.

Shelley gave an enormous sigh, partly from relief and partly from longing, and dropped into an easy chair. This was going to be tougher than she had thought.

Since Ross's hopes for a day spent with Shelley had come to naught, he decided to get some work done. That's why he was in Cincinnati in the first place, wasn't it? He might even take time out to consider the possibility that he was wrong — an activity he seldom wasted much time on once he'd decided what he wanted. It was possible that Shelley was right and that they should, for the sake of common sense and good business, call a halt to this thing between them before it even began.

Although he realized that adhering to Shelley's sense of duty would certainly make life simpler while he was here, Ross knew his life had never been simple, so why start now? Since she had made it clear she didn't want to see him the rest of the weekend, he expected to have plenty of time to consider all the angles of the problem tonight in his elegant, luxurious and very lonely hotel suite.

So much for the glamorous life, he thought wryly. Despite the long rest he'd taken the previous year, he was aware of feeling burned-out again. He was tired of changing cities — or even continents — every few months, tired of hotel rooms, plane flights, long-distance calls, sudden changes of plans. Oddly enough, despite his protests to Henri Montpazier, he still liked the work itself. At least he still liked the language schools, although he was tired of firing people and hoped he wouldn't have to do it again.

Parking downtown proved to be no problem on a Saturday. Elite, like Babel, was open on Saturdays to accommodate its students. The regular office staff didn't normally work weekends, however, so Ross was surprised to find Charles Winston-Clarke there. Charles was startled to see him, although his formal expression didn't really give much away. Ross greeted him politely and let himself into his own small, makeshift office, noting with amusement that Charles wore a suit and tie even on Saturdays.

Within minutes Ross was studying the school's financial records for the past year. He knew that central accounting had been complaining about the Cincinnati school for more than two years, and he had been given written and verbal briefings on the whole situation. The various financial logbooks were inconsistent and messy; the high turnover of staff at this school only further complicated matters. One accountant had even lost a vital logbook, and his successor had been forced to begin a new log in midyear with no record of the first six months.

And this was only one aspect of the job. As usual, Ross had his work cut out for him. However, things didn't look as bad as they had on his first job for Elite. That had been eight years ago in Toulouse. The assignment had been a bargain, a bet, really, between Henri Montpazier and a brash young man who had always rebelled against authority. Ross was older and calmer now, more experienced and more confident; he'd succeeded at this enough times to know he was very good at it. Perhaps that was why he wasn't concerned with his job this morning nearly as much as he was concerned with Michelle Baird.

Shelley.

Ross leaned back in his chair and closed his eyes briefly.

Perhaps if he'd been more alert, he would have made the connection sooner. He had known that the director of the Babel Language Center was negotiating with Keene International, and he had assumed she would be at their reception. But from the instant he'd noticed those big gray eyes staring at him with open interest, he'd been so taken by her that some of his brain cells had stopped working. Besides, what little he knew of the director of the Babel Language Center made him expect a brisk and aggressive businesswoman, which certainly didn't fit

Shelley's easy warmth and humor.

He smiled ruefully. The only thing about Shelley that fit in with his previous image of her were her simple, plain, even austere clothes. He supposed she dressed that way to make men keep their minds on business. It hadn't done any good in his case. He could picture her in velvet, in silk, in lace, in nothing at all. . . . He'd buy her something beautiful, something to go with her eyes, when he got to know her better.

If he got to know her better.

The memory of her kiss, the sweetness of her mouth, the feel of her full breasts pressing against his chest stirred inside him. She was so feminine, he mused, that she was like a fantasy of what a woman could be, and yet she had so many wonderful qualities that belied the myth of femininity as silly and helpless.

It was no wonder that so many businesses had contracted Shelley's services since her arrival in Cincinnati. She was lovely and intelligent, but even more than that, one immediately sensed her innate honesty and fairness. She would be a pleasure to do business with, someone you could trust. Her warmth and friendliness would reach out to clients, making them feel good about themselves and their potential for successfully adjusting to a new culture and a new language. Shelley could make people feel that Shelley would truly understand what they, their family, or their company needed from her school.

Ross's work had taught him how difficult it was to find good language school directors. He wondered where she had come from and what she had done before Babel.

"Ross, you seem lost in thought, *mon ami,*" said Charles, sticking his head inside Ross's cramped office.

Ross smiled faintly. Charles had obviously found out about his background. Born to an American father and a French mother, Ross was perfectly bilingual. Ever since his arrival two days earlier, Charles had been peppering his speech with French phrases pulled straight out of an Agatha Christie novel. It was an affectation Ross had encountered many times before. In this case he wasn't quite sure whether Charles was exhibiting awkward goodwill or a worn-out sense of humor, or was simply being a pompous idiot.

"Have a seat, Charles," Ross invited. As Charles slid clumsily into a chair, Ross wondered whether the middle-aged man had any facial expression other than the cool half smile he had been wearing since Ross's arrival.

"Finding everything you need?" Charles asked solicitously.

"Yes. You've been very helpful," Ross assured him, trying to detect some trace of animosity in Charles's expression. Since Ross's very presence at the school implied ineffectual management, and since his job might include firing Charles, he was prepared for resentment, even anger. It certainly wouldn't be the first time, he thought wearily. Charles, however, during Ross's first two days at the school, had been unfailingly courteous and cooperative, if understandably nervous. Ross had to appreciate the man's attitude.

"I'm afraid the books are in a terrible mess," said Charles apologetically. "We've had such an unexpectedly high turnover of staff here. I'm so hopelessly bad at bookkeeping that I don't even go near them myself. I can understand why the head office would object to that, of course. Perhaps I'll have to learn something about accounting after all. I'm afraid I'm just not a financially oriented man."

Ross fully intended to begin questioning Charles about some of the inconsistencies in the accounts, so he was rather surprised to hear himself say, "Tell me what you can about Michelle Baird."

"Michelle Baird?" Charles repeated with no change of expression.

"And the Babel Language Center," Ross added, feeling slightly ridiculous. He knew damn well that it wasn't strictly professional interest that had prompted his request. On the other hand, Shelley was not only the first thing on his mind at the moment, but she was also his chief competitor in this city, and Charles had known her professionally for over a year.

"She calls me Chuck," Charles said with the first flash of irritation Ross had seen in him.

Ross suppressed a smile. "What else?"

"What else does she call me?"

"What else do you know about her?" Ross clarified.

"She's single, twenty-eight years old, studied languages and linguistics at college, worked as a tour guide in Europe for several years after college and took a minor job with the Babel Center in Chicago when she came back to the US. Considering her lack of experience or qualifications, I really don't know how she got promoted to her current position. Of course, she's a very ambitious young woman, and quite pretty, too. Presumably she found a way to attract the attention of the man who was her immediate superior in Chicago. . . ." Charles trailed off, letting the innuendo dangle heavily between them.

Ross found the insinuation offensive when applied to the woman with whom he had hoped to spend the weekend. He reminded himself that this was a business discussion and considered the implications from that angle. Objectively he knew it was possible, but he was still skeptical; it would be foolish to put Babel's entire Cincinnati operation in the hands of a woman merely in payment for her favors. On the other hand, men were foolish over women with amazing regularity, particularly a woman as alluring as Shelley. Any sensible man who knew her intimately would no doubt quickly realize that it wouldn't be a mistake to put her in charge of a language school. . . .

Not liking the direction his thoughts were taking, Ross approached the question from another angle. "If she's so unqualified and inexperienced, how do you account for her frankly impressive success during her first year in this city?"

"How would you define success?" Charles asked with a touch of condescension.

"I define success as having virtually monopolized all new business within the past year, not to mention having drawn away some of our old clients," Ross said flatly.

"Well, if that's your only criterion for success —"

"Is there another one?" Ross challenged.

"Bien sûr," said Charles. Ross tried not to wince. "Surely professional integrity should be taken into consideration."

"Get to the point," Ross insisted.

"Miss Baird, as I have said, is a very attractive and ambitious young woman. . . ."

Ross spoiled Charles's dramatic pause. "Go on." He heard the harshness in his tone and reminded himself to be objective.

"I wouldn't want to be accused of spreading rumors, Ross," said Charles hesitantly.

"Nothing you say will go beyond these walls," Ross assured him. Confidentiality had always been part of his job, whether dealing with fact or fancy.

"Very well, then . . ."

Three

Relaxing that weekend would obviously be impossible, even impractical. All Shelley could do was sit around and wonder what Ross was doing — and whether or not it was too late to change her mind about spending the weekend with him.

So she threw herself into a frenzy of activity, cleaning the whole apartment, scrubbing down the kitchen, even braving the inside of her refrigerator, washing the car, running her errands, doing her laundry, writing to friends abroad and finally refinishing an old chair she'd acquired from her mother's basement on her last visit to Chicago.

By Monday morning she was exhausted enough to need another weekend to recuperate, but she still hadn't succeeded in banishing Ross Tanner from her thoughts.

She arrived at the office early Monday morning to organize the previous week's figures before the business day officially began. From nine o'clock onward, however, she was so busy that she finally asked Francesca to fax the figures to Jerome in Chicago and to have him fax her any information obtained on Ross Tanner. She wouldn't have time to study it until the evening.

Early in the morning students and teachers started arriving at the Babel Language Center. Shelley greeted everyone by name as they passed by her office or bumped into her near the coffeepot. She kept close track of her clients' progress. Although policy recommended that she make regular appointments with them, most clients got along well with Shelley and stopped by her office frequently for friendly, informal chats.

She liked to maintain close contact with Babel's staff of part-time teachers, too. Nearly everyone sat down with Shelley once a week or so to say hello and exchange news.

Pablo Gutierrez, a medical student from Venezuela, came into her office in a panic, explaining in frantic Spanish that he was having trouble with the immigration authorities even though his visa was valid. Shelley's own Spanish was rusty, since it was her fourth language — after English, French, and Italian — so she finally had to stop Pablo and insist he explain the situation in English.

She spent the next half hour on the telephone with various local government officials, finally agreeing to write letters on Pablo's behalf to the necessary authorities. It took nearly another half hour to assure Pablo that everything would be all right and that he had panicked unnecessarily.

After that, Mr. Powell entered her office. He was displeased with his progress in Greek and wanted to try another language.

"But, Mr. Powell," Shelley reminded him gently, "this will be the fourth language you've tried since your first visit here only five months ago."

"Don't misunderstand me, Shelley," Mr. Powell said immediately. "I am in no way complaining about the teachers or the Babel teaching method. I just don't seem to have a knack for Greek."

"Well, you felt that way about Spanish and French, as well. I don't think the problem is an inherent inability to learn any of these languages."

"Then why haven't I made any progress? I still have trouble saying the simplest little thing!" he said in frustration.

"Speaking another language is like playing a musical instrument," Shelley said patiently. "There isn't simply a theory you can look at and immediately put into use. I speak from experience when I say that in order to speak a language well, comfortably, fluidly and seemingly without effort, you must practice it for a long time, just as you would practice the piano for a long time before you would expect to play a Chopin nocturne without stopping every three measures."

"But I practice at home every night!"

"Mr. Powell, how long did it take you to learn to speak English?"

"I . . . well . . ."

"I would estimate that you were at least four or five years old before you became able to communicate on a sophisticated level with almost anyone. Although you're older and wiser now, you're less flexible than you were then, and you're attempting to learn a new language under artificial circumstances. You really need to give it at least a year before you start expecting to communicate without strain. Time and practice, Mr. Powell," Shelley concluded with an encouraging smile.

Mr. Powell mulled this over for a moment before his face broke into a wide grin. "In that case, Shelley, I'd like to go back to the French, which is what I came here to learn in the first place. It just sounds a lot prettier to me than this Greek stuff. No offense intended to the Greeks."

"And this time you'll stick with it?"

"Yes, this time I'll stick with it. I think," he added.

"All right, Mr. Powell. You tell Francesca when you want to have your lessons this week, and we'll call you later today after we've booked a teacher."

"Thank you, Shelley."

After Mr. Powell's departure, Shelley recalled with amusement that he conducted decision-making seminars for top-level businessmen all over the Midwest.

"Shelley," Francesca said, sticking her head into Shelley's momentarily silent office. "Washington is on the line."

"Washington?"

"Coordinator of interpreters."

"Oh, right," Shelley said dispiritedly.

"*Vuoi un po' di caffè?*" Francesca asked.

"Yes, coffee would be wonderful, thank you, Francesca." She picked up the phone. "Hello?"

"Shelley, it's about that job for the courts next week . . . Have you found an interpreter yet for the witness?"

"No, not yet."

"No? No!" the woman said accusingly. "Why not, may I ask?"

"I'm in Cincinnati, remember?" Shelley said patiently. "Where do you expect me to find a native speaker of Pashto who speaks English fluently enough to give simultaneous translations in legal proceedings, and who happens to be a U.S. citizen, too? You don't just find hordes of people from Afghanistan standing around in Fountain Square waving their citizenship papers in your face."

"Well, have you made any effort at all?"

"Of course, I've made an effort. I'm still making an effort," Shelley said, beginning to dislike the new coordinator. It was evidently a nerve-racking job, since no one had lasted in it more than six months.

"May I inquire what effort?" the woman said with venomous sweetness."

"I've contacted the Islamic Association of Cincinnati, the foreign students' organization of every college in southern Ohio, Traveler's Aid, Immigration and every Middle Eastern restaurant in town. Since I only received your message Friday afternoon, I think it's fair to say I gave it considerable attention before the weekend began," Shelley replied, her patience becoming a little forced.

"If you *fail* to find someone, you could jeopardize a very important contract, my dear," the woman warned.

Shelley winced at the word "fail" and scowled at the words "my dear."

"If there is an American Pashto speaker in all of Cincinnati, I will find him and, if necessary, I will personally drag him kicking and screaming to the law courts. Satisfied?" she said with barely concealed annoyance.

"Just find one. I'll phone again tomorrow," the woman said, and hung up.

The phone rang again almost immediately. Shelley regarded it with loathing.

"Shelley," Francesca said as she carried a cup of coffee in, "some of that information from Jerome in Chicago is coming through now on the telefax machine."

"All right."

"Aren't you going to answer the phone?"

"Let Wayne get it."

"Wayne is on the line to New York."

"Well, then you get it."

"I am making more coffee."

Shelley sighed and reluctantly picked up the phone. "Babel Language Center. Can I help you?"

"Shelley, this is Mike Paige over at Keene International."

"Hello, Mike. How are you?" Shelley took a deep breath and crossed her fingers. He was the man she'd been negotiating with for Keene's sizable contract.

"Shelley, you may have heard that there's a new man over at the Elite Language Center, a guy named Ross Tanner. Well, he came in and spoke with my superior this morning, who was very impressed with him. So it looks like we may be much farther from a decision than I thought."

"I see," Shelley said. Ross certainly worked fast, didn't he? She was disturbed but maintained a calm tone. "Does your boss still want me to meet with him tomorrow?"

"Oh, yes, certainly —"

"But?" Shelley asked, sensing the man was debating a whether or not to tell her something else.

"But he wants me to meet with Tanner tomorrow to see what I think of the man's proposal."

"Oh."

"I'm telling you this because I like you, Shelley. I was hoping we'd go with your school. Maybe we still will."

"I intend to do my best to see that you do," Shelley said brightly. "Thanks for calling, Mike."

"Shelley," Francesca called just as she was putting down the receiver. "Can you come out here please?"

Shelley went into the hallway, where a delivery man was quickly pulling up a dozen or more large boxes.

"What's going on here?" Shelley demanded.

"Rush delivery, ma'am. Got the order Friday."

"Delivery of what?"

Francesca examined the packing lists. "Mandarin grammar books," she informed Shelley.

"*All* of them?"

"I think so, Shelley."

"What's going on here?" said Wayne, coming out into the hallway.

"Who ordered this?" Shelley asked.

"School number 112, ma'am. It says so right there on the receipt," the deliveryman said.

"School number 112?" Wayne repeated. "That's in —"

"Los Angeles," Shelley finished. "There's been a mistake. We're school number 121."

"No mistake, ma'am. Your address is listed right here."

Shelley looked at his list. It was their address, all right.

"Someone in distribution has really messed up. Francesca, get on the phone to LA. Tell them we've got their books." She noticed the deliveryman starting to leave. "Wait, where are you going?"

"Got other deliveries to make, ma'am."

"Can you take these books with you? They're not ours."

"What should I do with them?"

Wayne's eyes met Shelley's. "I wouldn't touch that line with a ten-foot pole if I were you," he warned.

Shelley noticed for the first time that Wayne was holding a thick sheaf of papers. "Is that the information Jerome sent from Chicago?" she asked suddenly.

"Yes. You'd better have a look at this when you get a chance." He handed the stack of papers to her. "Jerome says we definitely have a problem on our hands. Tanner looks like a clever devil."

Shelley held the papers as if they might burn her fingers. "All right, as soon as I get a chance," she said in a low voice.

"Excuse me, ma'am, but just where do you expect me to put these books?" asked the deliveryman plaintively.

"Maybe you could take them back to your loading dock. Just get them out of my hallway. They're blocking the way and are probably causing a fire hazard." Shelley frowned as she took a cursory glance through the accumulated information about Ross's career.

"I have other deliveries to make, ma'am, I can't —"

The front door opened again. Shelley glanced up, hoping it wouldn't be a new client walking in to find chaos reigning at her language center. She, Wayne, Francesca, and the deliveryman bickering over a dozen boxes of Mandarin grammar books wouldn't present a picture of keen professionalism.

It was worse than a new client.

"Ross!" she exclaimed.

"Hello, Shelley. I hope I haven't come at a bad time," he said diplomatically as he surveyed the confusion.

Wayne stopped arguing with the deliveryman and gaped at Ross. "Ross Tanner?" he asked incredulously.

"Yes. Word travels fast around here, doesn't it? Makes me feel terribly welcome, like one of the family already. You must be Wayne Thompson?" Ross said pleasantly, simply oozing upper-crust charm.

For once Wayne was robbed of speech. He just nodded dumbly and accepted Ross's proffered hand.

Francesca's eyes widened when she recognized Ross. Although she kept sending Shelley meaningful glances, she was on the telephone to the Babel school in Los Angeles and couldn't take time out to comment.

"What are you doing here?" Shelley asked Ross in confusion.

"Yeah," said Wayne with a regrettable lack of couth.

Ross looked briefly at Wayne, a subtly assessing glance, before saying to Shelley, "There's a business matter I'd like to discuss with you."

"Business?" Shelley repeated blankly. He was a competitor, not a client. "What kind of business?"

"It's . . . delicate. I would prefer to discuss it in private."

"Ma'am, I need to get going," said the hapless deliveryman.

"You can't just leave behind a dozen boxes of Mandarin grammar books that don't belong to me," Shelley argued. "Just wait a few minutes and we'll sort this out with the LA school. Please." She turned back to

Ross. "I'm awfully busy —"

"You should have made an appointment," Wayne said as if he had just found a clever loophole.

"Considering the rather hostile relationship between the Babel and Elite schools in Cincinnati, I suspected your appointment calendar might be full if I called ahead," Ross said.

Shelley clutched the report about Ross to her chest, feeling absurdly guilty about it. "We certainly wouldn't refuse you an appointment just because we're competitors," she said with dignity. "If you'll give me a few minutes to sort this out, then we can go into my office to discuss your business."

"Great. I'll just have a seat over here," Ross said agreeably.

Shelley deplored the seats in the lobby, since they were squat and uncomfortable, and most people looked ridiculous sitting down on them. Ross, however, slid onto his chair with graceful ease and lounged there like an indolent panther, watching them all with an enigmatic expression that Shelley suspected concealed vast amusement.

She, Wayne, Francesca, and even the deliveryman stared at him as if they were waiting for his permission to go about their business.

"Don't mind me," he said politely. He settled back and let his eyes rest on Shelley.

"Shelley," Francesca said suddenly, "the director in LA says he hasn't ordered any Mandarin books."

"What? Give me that," Shelley said, taking the phone from Francesca.

"Hello, this is Shelley Baird," she said into the receiver. "Well, your school number is on all of the boxes. Yes. School number 112 . . . . But it must be your number. It's always been your number."

Shelley looked up as two more people came into the lobby. She heard one of them, a young blond man with a Scandinavian accent, tell Wayne they were from the foreign students' union at a local college.

"Just a minute," Shelley said into the receiver. She introduced herself to the blond boy who had spoken. "Have you found a Pashto speaker?" she asked eagerly.

"Yes. Right here," said the boy proudly.

"Great! Let me finish this and I'll be right with you." She spoke into the receiver again. "I'm sorry, what were you saying? Oh . . . Oh. I see. Well, why did they do that? I see. All right. Well, thanks for your help, we'll get right on it."

Shelley hung up the phone and turned to Francesca. "For reasons no one understands, headquarters changed the numbers of all the schools out west last week. LA thinks those books are supposed to go to Portland, Oregon, but he says we'd better call first and ask. Will you please do that, Francesca?"

"Excuse me, ma'am," said the delivery man, "but I can't wait around —"

"Where are you going on your vacation this year?" Shelley asked him suddenly.

"What?"

"Your vacation. Where are you going?"

"Well . . . Mexico."

"Aha! Sir, if you'll wait around till we find out where those boxes are going, and if you'll then get them out of here, we'll give you three complimentary Spanish lessons."

"Well, I . . . Three free lessons, did you say?"

"Absolutely. Just think of it. You'll be able to check into your hotel, order food in restaurants, ask directions, and barter over prices. You can eliminate all the normal hassles of a tourist in a foreign culture. *If* you'll just give me a hand here."

"I can learn all that in just three lessons?" the deliveryman asked dubiously.

"I give you my personal guarantee," Shelley assured him. "We offer private lessons with the most modern, intensive, successful instruction in the field."

The man hesitated for another moment, weighing his options. Finally he said, "Well, I like your face, ma'am. I don't think you'd try to snow me. You've got a deal."

"Thank you," said Shelley, shaking his hand enthusiastically. "Wayne, will you please get this gentleman three lesson vouchers and arrange his times? Now," Shelley said, turning to her newly found Pashto speaker, "let me explain the situation to you, sir. I'm Shelley Baird."

Shelley offered her hand to the man. He stared at her uncertainly for a moment before taking it in a brief handshake. She waited for him to offer his name. When he didn't, she finally said, "I'm afraid I didn't get your name."

He stared at her.

Shelley looked uncertainly at the blond boy, then back to the Afghan man. "What is your name?" she asked clearly.

"Hmm?"

"Do you speak English?" Shelley asked slowly.

The man smiled shyly and responded, "Are with numb English."

Shelley felt disappointed but not entirely surprised. She had been through false starts before when looking for interpreters of unusual languages. As she had told the coordinator in Washington, she wouldn't find someone overnight. Nevertheless, she didn't appreciate having her time wasted. She turned again to the blond young man.

"Didn't I specifically say that I need an Afghan who is an American citizen and speaks fluent English?" she said patiently.

"Well, his English is a little slow —"

"It's a little non-existent. If he can't tell me his name, how do you expect him to give accurate simultaneous interpretation of complicated legal language?"

"Well, perhaps . . ."

"And where are his citizenship papers?"

"Um."

"I appreciate your help," Shelley said diplomatically, "but my instructions were clear and specific. If you ignore them, I'm afraid you simply waste your time and energy. Not to mention my own."

The boy sighed. "I'm sorry, Miss Baird. We thought it might be good enough that he spoke Pashto. Better luck next time, eh?"

Shelley smiled politely, not wanting to offend someone who possessed good intentions, even if they were misdirected. Besides, he might be able to help her in the future.

Shelley showed them to the door, then turned to face Ross. His eyes watched her with an intense interest that she sensed was purely professional in this instance. She resented his presence during such a chaotic day, not wishing him to see her operation at anything less than peak efficiency. On the other hand, he of all people should know that this was a complex business that seldom provided a calm — or dull — day.

Francesca was on the phone to Portland, making arrangements to ship them their Chinese books. Wayne was shuffling some papers on Francesca's desk, a transparent excuse for staying in the lobby to study Ross. Ross was totally unperturbed by Wayne's ill-concealed interest in him, and he returned Francesca's glances with a flattering, slightly flirtatious expression.

He certainly did dress up the lobby, Shelley reflected.

The door opened again behind Shelley. She turned to see a German teacher enter the arena.

"*Guten Tag,* Shelley," the woman said.

"*Guten Tag, Ute. Wie geht's?*"

"*Was ist das?*" Ute asked, surveying the disorder in the hallway.

"It's a long story," Shelley said. "You're very early today, aren't you?"

"*Ja.* I have come early because I must speak with you about something."

Shelley glanced at her watch, hoping she would have time for both Ute and Ross before her next appointment arrived. "Of course, Ute. I have agreed to see this gentleman first, if you don't mind waiting."

Ute looked at Ross. Her expression reflected what Shelley had come to accept as a normal female reaction to his presence. Although Ute was a married woman awaiting the arrival of her third grandchild, her face lit up with a fascinated smile as she introduced herself to Ross. He stood up and took Ute's hand.

"*Sehr erfreut. Ich bin* Ross Tanner," he said, surprising Shelley.

"*So,*" Ute said with interest, "*Sie sind Herr Tanner. Wie geht es Ihnen?*"
"*Danke gut. Und Ihnen?*"

"Shelley," Francesca interrupted. "Portland wants to speak to you. They say they didn't order Mandarin books. They ordered Cantonese books."

Shelley sighed and took the receiver. While she talked with the director of the Portland school and patiently explained that the mistake wasn't her fault and she didn't know who was responsible, she was aware of Ute and Ross carrying on an animated conversation nearby. Shelley had already demonstrated the extent of her German vocabulary, so she had no idea what they were saying. Ross's German was obviously quite fluent, and she wondered where he had learned it. She had the impression that that was what Ute was asking him.

"Yes, I've examined the contents of the boxes. According to the English on the cover, they're definitely Mandarin and not Cantonese," Shelley told the distressed director in Portland. "Well, I'll send these back to distribution. You'd better give them a call and explain the problem. No, I don't know why these things always happen to you."

Shelley hung up the phone with a rueful smile. However bad her day was, it sounded as if the director in Portland was having a worse one. Shelley shook her head. She really liked this job, but she hated the bureaucracy involved in such a big organization.

Once off the phone, Shelley caught Ross's eye. They'd better get this conversation under way before something else happened. He tore himself away from an enamored Ute, evidently saying he had enjoyed chatting with her, and followed Shelley into her office.

Shelley sat at her desk and put the faxed report about Ross Tanner behind her, out of view. She had intended to be all business, but curiosity got ahold of her.

"Where did you learn to speak German so well?" she asked.

"I worked in the Elite school in Munich early in my career."

"What other languages do you speak?"

"French and Arabic. The French doesn't really count, though. I was raised bilingual. My mother's French. I spent a lot of my childhood over there."

"I see," Shelley said thoughtfully. That would probably explain his educated, carefully neutral accent, particularly if he spent most of that time in France among friends and relatives who didn't speak English.

"You look lovely today," he said with a suddenly personal tone of voice, his blue eyes curiously wistful.

"You look quite . . . well, you know . . . you always do."

"Thank you, I think," he said dryly.

Shelley cleared her throat nervously. She had a sudden, alarmingly clear picture of the two of them locked in each other's arms on Saturday morning. She couldn't have something like that happening here in her office.

"I thought you said you came here to discuss business," she said tersely.

"Actually, I did. I just find you so distracting"

"Sublimate," she suggested.

"Very well."

Ross tilted his head to one side and studied her for a moment. An aura of feminine sexuality surrounded her, even in a business setting. She could certainly use it to her advantage, as Charles had intimated, yet it seemed to be quite unconscious and natural. Charles had suggested — no, specifically stated — that Shelley used *all* her attributes in a most unprofessional way to ensure her professional success. Since that was a type of competition that Charles obviously wouldn't enter into, it could explain Shelley's remarkable success this past year and exonerate Charles.

If it were true, Ross wouldn't have to fire Charles and thus throw a middle-aged man out of work. Yet the thought of Shelley behaving as Charles claimed disturbed him far more than he cared to acknowledge. Now, looking at this small woman with her ivory skin, her tumbling copper hair and her candid gray eyes, he felt stronger, more compelling needs stir inside him. He desperately wanted her to convince him it wasn't true.

He felt caught in the middle, confused and uncertain. This was all the more disturbing because it was unfamiliar and uncharacteristic. In the past he had been headstrong, rebellious, selfish, and careless, but never indecisive. Could he be losing his touch? He frowned, willing himself to take charge of the situation, to use that combination of ruthlessness and charm that had always been his strength.

Shelley watched Ross curiously for a moment, aware he was fighting some sort of an internal battle. She wasn't vain enough to assume he was having that much trouble sublimating his attraction to her, so she watched carefully for some clue about his dilemma. It must involve her, or he wouldn't be here.

A subtle change came over him in that moment. When he spoke again his tone was polite and had lost all trace of intimacy. His eyes flattered her, but they were no longer warm and admiring.

"I've come across evidence of some rather unprofessional disagreements between you and Charles," he said.

Shelley narrowed her eyes. "Is this about the time I swore out a peace bond on him?"

"Peace bond?" Ross heard the obvious surprise in his own voice.

"Ahh," said Shelley, "I can see it's not. He managed to keep that a secret, didn't he?"

Years of experience made Ross recover his *sangfroid* almost immediately. "Perhaps you'd like to tell me about it."

"I called the police because I felt Chuck had really gone too far that time, and I didn't want to deal with it myself."

Ross suddenly had a feeling this conversation wasn't going to be anything like what he'd planned. "What do you mean?" he asked slowly.

"There were other incidents, of course."

"Such as?" Ross asked coolly. His mind was working furiously as he listened to Shelley with an expression of polite interest.

"Well, shortly after I first arrived and started picking up new business, Chuck started making crank phone calls to my office day in and day out. It got to the point where we didn't even want to answer the phone anymore."

"What makes you think it was him?" Ross said with apparent skepticism.

"I mentioned it to him one day when I saw him having lunch in a restaurant near here. One look in his eyes and I knew he was responsible for it," she said with certainty.

"That's sheer speculation," Ross said critically.

"I also thought I recognized his voice. What's more, our office opens an hour earlier than Elite and stays open an hour later, but we only got these calls during Elite's business hours."

"That can hardly be considered evidence," Ross argued.

"No, I realize that. But I walked over to Chuck's office the next day and told him that if I received one more crank phone call from *anyone,* I'd call the police and report him. End of crank calls."

Ross absorbed this in silence for a moment. "I see," he said slowly. "But that doesn't —"

"Then, believe it or not, Chuck started sending spies over here. Once every two or three weeks, someone would make an appointment with me, then demand to see every inch of the school and ask all sorts of detailed questions that had nothing to do with language tuition. They were pretty easy to spot, and even easier to get rid of, but I was getting awfully annoyed."

"Frankly, I'm afraid I find that as unlikely as the crank phone calls," Ross said, attempting to regain control of the conversation. "Surely the police didn't issue a peace bond based on your vague suspicions."

Shelley felt somehow hurt for a moment that he was so skeptical of her convictions. But he was the man from Elite, and that was exactly why she had decided not to get involved with him.

"No, of course not. Last October I signed another big client Chuck had been after. He made all sorts of threats — privately, where no one else could hear him — about ruining my business. Then someone broke in here one night."

"Broke in?" Ross exclaimed. This was serious.

Shelley nodded. "They didn't take any money or valuable materials, but they did take my client address book, my list of teachers' phone numbers and — get this — my schedule board. It took us two weeks to get everything back to normal efficiency."

"That was when you called the police?" Ross had to wonder why Charles hadn't mentioned any of these unpleasant incidents to him while he'd been defaming Shelley's character on Saturday.

"Yes. I asked them to pay him a visit. I swore out a peace bond on him and made it very clear he'd be in trouble with the law if he ever came near me or my school again."

"My God," Ross breathed, staring at Shelley. He had intended to subtly but stringently question her until he had satisfied himself about the truth or falsehood of Charles's accusations. All he had now were more accusations, this time aimed at his own employee. And Shelley's accusations were largely as vague and as difficult to confirm as Charles's.

"Have there been any other . . . problems you'd like to tell me about?" he asked. If she would offer something he could easily prove or disprove . . .

Shelley's cheeks reddened slightly as she considered whether or not to tell him about Chuck's latest offense, "It's . . . quite embarrassing, actually. I haven't mentioned it to anyone else. Maybe . . . well, you're his boss, Ross, am you're obviously a gentleman. Maybe you can tell him to knock it off."

"What?" he prodded. He was far less a gentleman than Shelley realized, but that was suddenly something he didn't think he wanted her to know about him.

"Mike Paige of Keene International confided to me that Chuck insinuated that I offer . . . after-hours favors to men, to clients I mean, to get them to sign contracts and pay bid money. He implied that I didn't know how to run a language school but had . . . slept my way into this position." She was relieved to see Ross's eyes widen in surprise. At least he believed her this time. "You can imagine, I'm sure, how humiliating that is. Fortunately Mike didn't believe a word of it, and I know it won't go any further. But I shudder to think how many other people Chuck may have said that to. I mean . . . for God's sake, Ross!"

He stood up quite abruptly. For the first time since Shelley had met him, he looked openly agitated. He rubbed a hand across his face, started to speak, stopped himself, then thrust his hands into his pockets and looked away from her with a dark, brooding frown.

She saw confusion, anger, and surprise in his face. She waited for him to apologize for his employee's behavior, assure her it wouldn't happen again, make some personal gesture of comfort or commiseration.

He simply stood there, however, looking dark and unapproachable, looking like a total stranger, neither the charming flirt, nor the polite businessman nor the teasingly tender suitor she'd seen in him. He looked like the formidable and ruthless man Henri Montpazier had hired to strengthen Elite's worldwide business empire and to eliminate all obstacles to success.

She suddenly knew that he hadn't come here to hear her complaints about Chuck or to propose a friendly yet businesslike relationship between their companies. With a sinking heart and an inexplicable feeling of betrayal, she stood and drew herself up to her full height.

"Why did you come here today?" she asked quietly.

His eyes met hers. He realized there was no point in denying anything. She obviously knew. She was too damned quick for her own good. He merely nodded, confirming her suspicions.

"How dare you?" she said with growing fury.

"I didn't come here to accuse you of anything," he protested wearily. "I simply came to find out if it was true."

"Why would you believe it even for a moment?" she challenged.

"Because it would explain a lot of things."

She felt as if he'd slapped her. "Explain what? How I managed to get this job? How I run a successful business with a growing clientele in a city where my only competition is a dishonest, incompetent, under-handed slime-puppy like Chuck?"

"Shelley, don't —"

"You obviously have a very high opinion of my capabilities," she continued sarcastically, "to think for even a moment that I would sleep around to get a job, to get clients. And to think that I would need to! As if I had no intelligence, no self-respect, no business acumen, no integrity —"

She broke off suddenly, and stared at him with wide, shocked eyes. "Is *that* what you were doing the day we met?"

"No!" he cut in forcefully. "Stop —"

"Is that why you came to my apartment? To see if it was true? To see if you could get some *entertainment* while you confirmed Chuck's preposterous stories about me?"

"Sit down and listen to me," he said firmly.

"Get out of my office."

"Shelley, this has nothing to do with how we met or what happened between us in your apartment. I hadn't even talked to Chuck yet," he said, unconsciously using her nickname for the man.

"Oh, well, that makes ail the difference!"

"Will you try to think objectively?" he snapped. "I'm new in town, I hardly know you, I don't know Chuck at all. As my employee he offered one possible explanation about why your business has been so much better than ours ever since you came to town. It's my job to investigate that possibility. It's not personal. It's got nothing to do with us," he insisted.

"Of *course* it's personal, and there is no 'us'! Do you think I can hear an accusation like that and simply forget about it when I go home at the end of the day, not caring who else heard it or might believe it? Do you think I can feel anything but embarrassed about kissing you on Saturday, knowing that it was so casual to you that you seriously considered Chuck's accusations about me?"

Feeling surprisingly defensive and a little ashamed, he retaliated. "I think you've met Chuck blow for blow when it comes to accusations, Shelley. And yours can't be proven any more easily than his can."

There was an unbearably tense silence between them. Shelley was shocked at them both. She so seldom lost her temper that her entire system felt unbalanced. He had hurt her. She was disgusted with herself for allowing him that kind of access to her emotions and furious with him for doing it. As if they realized in the same moment that things were getting out of hand, they both sat down and composed themselves.

"All right, Ross," she said with forced calm. "If you want to regard my experiences as unfounded accusations while you deem Chuck's insulting stories to be worthy of investigation, that's your choice. But I will continue to take it personally, and I don't want to see you again under any circumstances."

"Look," he began, wanting to prevent an ultimatum like that, "we need to talk —"

"What's more, I'll give you something you can investigate. Chuck's salary can't be much more than mine, yet he owns a house in Hyde Park, drives a Mercedes and vacationed in Japan last year. Since he's not independently wealthy and hasn't won the lottery recently, and since your profits in Cincinnati have fallen off while he's been the director here, surely a smart fellow like you can figure out that there must be a connection."

"How do you know all this?" he demanded.

"There are very few secrets around here, Ross. Besides, it's written all over his face," she added with certainty. "But I wouldn't want to bore you with any more of my unfounded accusations. If you'll excuse me, I have a business to run."

He sighed. "Okay, I'll go quietly, officer." She didn't smile. "I know I've offended you, but . . . Oh, hell. Look, can we talk about this? Can I call you tonight?"

"I'm busy tonight."

"Really?" He had caught the note of challenge in her voice.

"Yes. You see, Mr. Tanner, my Chicago office just sent me a big pile of information today. About you. And it looks like I'll need the whole evening to go over it. It seems you've been a very busy man."

Ross regarded the sheaf of papers with hooded eyes. His life in black and white. He could guess what she would find there. Nothing very reassuring from her point of view, that much was certain.

"Perhaps you're right," he conceded. "Maybe we should forget the whole thing."

"Yes, that's the only thing to do," she agreed hollowly.

"Have a nice evening, Shelley. I hope it makes fascinating reading."

He stood with his usual grace. Shelley rose to open the door. He brushed by her and stopped suddenly to look down at her. She looked up at him, feeling small and feminine and, for some reason, desirable. She took a shallow breath and felt an overwhelming urge to touch him. Her skin suddenly burned so much she felt he must surely notice the heat. His gaze dropped to the rapid rise and fall of her breasts, and a hungry expression stole over his face with surprising force. A silent, primitive message passed between them, and he suddenly seemed very wild, standing there in his expensive suit. Danger and excitement coursed through Shelley. She knew beyond a shadow of a doubt that he was about to crush her in his arms, ignore her sensible protests, and kiss her till her soul melted. She could hardly wait. She leaned forward to encourage him.

Then, as if she had imagined that sudden moment of desire between them, Ross broke free of the spell surrounding them. "Thanks for your time," he murmured, and walked out of her office. She trailed after him into the lobby. Francesca, Wayne, and Ute all looked at them with intense curiosity. Shelley wondered whether desire was an aura that people could see.

Ross politely said goodbye and left. Shelley held herself together by force of will. She wanted to run after him, tell him she'd changed her mind, that she'd go somewhere quiet and romantic with him — somewhere a thousand miles from work and distractions and responsibilities. Shelley went back to her office and tried to concentrate, but she couldn't shake her dissatisfaction and disappointment. What had she expected?

Except for the obvious fact that she simply wasn't a *femme fatale*, why shouldn't he investigate Chuck's accusations? Could he have trusted her implicitly in favor of his own employee? This all was a clever if rather obvious ploy on Chuck's part; such a situation would certainly exonerate Chuck for all blame for losing new business to her. Ross had been trying to do his job. She wondered whether she had lowered her credibility by playing the woman scorned. She couldn't help it. After the instant rapport between them on Friday, after the special passion between them on Saturday, how could he have doubted her character for a moment?

She glanced at the report on him, feeling suddenly sheepish. She doubted him, didn't she? She was checking up on him, just the way he was checking up on her. The only difference was that the rumors he had heard about her were insulting and sordid, whereas what she had heard about him was alarming and intimidating. Perhaps she should have agreed to let him call her so they could talk it over.

No, it was best to put a stop to it before it began. She was a sensible adult and a responsible professional, and she would have to master this attraction she felt for a business competitor.

So stop feeling like you've just lost your best friend, dummy, she chided herself silently.

She picked up the report on Ross. She was dying to know what it said, yet she was as loath to touch it as if it were a venomous snake. She was tentatively leafing through it when Ute stuck her head into her office and asked whether she finally had a moment to see her.

"Yes, of course, Ute," Shelley said, annoyed with herself for forgetting the woman had come early specifically to talk to her.

Shelley sat down and spent a moment composing herself so she could give Ute her full attention. Then she asked the woman what was on her mind.

"I want a raise or I'm quitting," Ute said in a rush.

Shelley had sensed this coming for a while but was sorry to hear it nonetheless. "Ute, you know that pay scales are decided upon by the New York office. I have already recommended you for a raise —"

"Perhaps you can ask again."

They discussed Ute's demand for several minutes. Shelley listened sympathetically, particularly because she agreed that Babel underpaid its teachers. Although most of them were part-time workers, they were the backbone of the language schools. Big international organizations like Babel and Elite, however, had such enormous overhead that they had to cut corners somewhere. Shelley thought her superiors made a mistake in assuming that good language teachers who were willing to work for low wages at odd hours were in plentiful supply. What's more, native speakers were particularly difficult to find in Cincinnati, a small midwestern city with a limited foreign population.

"I understand your position, Ute, and will try to influence my superiors at headquarters." She smiled encouragingly but she was secretly pessimistic about her chances. Headquarters maintained an inflexible policy about pay scales. "In the meantime, Ute, I have new clients that I'm sure you'll enjoy teaching. They're a group of engineers being transferred to West Germany, and they want to begin lessons soon and study as much as possible before their departure. I'm counting on you. I'm short two German teachers since the Schmidts went back to Munich last month," she added hesitantly.

"You will tell me what headquarters says. Then I will tell you if I will be here any longer."

"All right, Ute."

The German woman shrugged in frustration. "I like you very much. I like the job very much, and the hours are very convenient for me. But it is a question of respect and fairness, Shelley."

"I understand, Ute," Shelley said, feeling caught in the middle.

After Ute had left her office, Shelley looked at her watch and realized she only had a few minutes before her next appointment. She picked up a stone-cold cup of coffee, which had been sitting on her desk since Francesca had brought it to her ages ago, and stirred it around, feeling dispirited.

Some days at this job were wonderful, and other days . . . "Well," she said aloud.

She was walking down the hallway to get a fresh cup of coffee when an unbearably spine-chilling, blood-curdling, ear-splitting noise erupted throughout the building.

Wayne came charging into the hallway with his hands over his ears. All the doors along the hall opened as teachers and students peered down the corridor or cried out in alarm.

"What in the blazes is that?" exclaimed Wayne.

"Fire alarm," said Shelley tiredly.

It just wasn't her day.

Four

*T*hat evening Shelley sat curled up in an easy chair in her apartment with a big mug of coffee and the report on Ross Tanner. The report did indeed make fascinating reading, particularly when coupled with notes Wayne had taken during his conversation with an informative friend in New York who had once worked for Elite.

Shelley figured her mother would refer to Ross as a remittance man. Ross's father was one of the five hundred richest men in America, a wealthy banker with international holdings. His mother came from an old family in Provence. He had two sisters, both of whom had married men of the same exalted social and financial status. Ross clearly made

a good living at Elite but, as the family outcast, he had given up a
birthright of vast wealth, power, and influence.

His life until Elite seemed like a series of false starts. He had been
thrown out of three expensive private schools during his youth. Jerome's
report offered no specific cause for those expulsions, though Wayne's
friend vaguely said it was because he'd been incorrigible. He had
evidently wound up finishing his education in France before returning
to the U.S. for college.

Wayne's scrawled notes indicated that Ross's family's influence had
overcome his erratic grades and terrible reputation, and he'd enrolled
in the exclusive Ivy League college that his father and grandfather before
him had attended. He had majored in medieval Middle Eastern philosophy, a major he'd invented himself and somehow talked his professors into accrediting. Shelley grinned, realizing that he must have done
it just to foil another of his family's attempts to make him fit the mold.
That must be when he began learning Arabic, too.

Predictably, he had been thrown out in the middle of his sophomore
year. Shelley frowned as she sifted through the garbled information
about his collegiate adventures. Initially his family had been able to
soothe the university's anger about Ross's pranks, rebelliousness, sloppy
work, and infrequent attendance. Naturally there were escapades with
women, too. It was sheer speculation, of course, since the facts had been
suppressed by his family, but Ross had apparently got himself involved
with a female faculty member who was supposed to be above such
shenanigans.

Shelley sipped her coffee and considered this. Yes, even at nineteen,
Ross must have possessed enormous sexual magnetism. Giving him the
benefit of the doubt, Shelley supposed the older woman in question
had been at least equally responsible for their entanglement. Shelley
doubted he'd been innocent even at that age, but everything about his
life until then implied he wouldn't have yet possessed the unflappable
savoir-faire that made him so devastating. He must have been quite
endearing in those days — in a thoroughly exasperating way.

She returned her attention to the report. Finally Ross had done
something even his family couldn't smooth over, and he was expelled.
The official reason was destruction of university property and disrup-
tion of classes; he had used the chemistry lab to concoct a mysterious
aphrodisiac he'd read about in his studies. Inhalation of the substance
caused immediate euphoria, followed by about twelve hours of uncon-
sciousness. A number of wildly euphoric students and professors had
done considerable damage to the hallowed halls of the building before
sleeping it off for a day. The fumes didn't fade for three days, so classes
had had to be rescheduled or cancelled. The incident had been widely
written about. It had even made the national evening news, since it was

rather amusing and involved both an exclusive university and a boy from a prominent family.

My, my, Shelley thought wryly, never a dull moment. His parents must have been livid. If they had attempted to enroll him in any other colleges, there was no evidence of it. Ross's educational career was over.

The information, both official and unofficial, became vague at that point. Large gaps of time were unaccounted for, and even Wayne's source could only offer vague, half-remembered rumors about this period of Ross's life.

Whether the family had cut him off or he'd simply deserted them wasn't quite clear, but it was apparent that he had no contact with them for quite some time. He dropped out of sight for several years.

It was believed that he had spent considerable time in North Africa, and rumor had him involved in everything from smuggling to espionage. There was no doubt, however, that he had managed a casino in Marrakech for a while.

Shelley's eyes widened as she tried to picture Ross in this exotic lifestyle. It would have been very hard on a spoiled, high-spirited, sheltered society boy, no matter how adventurous and rebellious he'd been. She guessed that it was during this period that he'd acquired the strength of character and self-confidence that lived under the surface of his charm and elegance.

He'd eventually resurfaced in Nice where he had managed a nightclub for a while. Shelley recalled that his mother's family came from that area and wondered whether he had chosen to live closer to loved ones.

He quit the job in Nice and wound up in Paris. That was where he had met Henri Montpazier — and so began his career with Elite.

At this point the information on Ross's career was extremely specific and thoroughly alarming. The man had the Midas touch. He had been twenty-six years old, a college dropout with a shady past, when Henri Montpazier had sent him to the Elite school in Toulouse. Montpazier had given him a free hand, a big expense account, and one year to change the school from an albatross into the goose that laid the golden egg.

Ross must have known next to nothing about running a language school, Shelley reasoned, yet by the end of the year the school was turning an enormous profit and their only competition had been forced to close down.

That experience laid the pattern for Ross's career with Elite. Montpazier had given him a huge bonus and immediately sent him to Munich. It had taken Ross just over ten months to set things straight there. His next assignment, in Hong Kong, had lasted barely nine months. He was learning fast and getting better each time.

His travels read like a whirlwind tour of thrilling cities. Over the next four years he'd worked in New York, Los Angeles, Bangkok, Berlin,

Milan, Sydney, Rio de Janeiro, Riyadh, Tokyo and Zurich. It was no wonder that now Ross, at thirty-four, had no wife or family. Shelley doubted he'd ever been in one place long enough to acquire even a goldfish.

Eighteen months ago he'd simply disappeared again. He'd quit and left Elite with no word about where he was going or what he intended to do. Wayne's source said that Henri Montpazier practically thought of Ross as his own son and was hurt by this behavior. For whatever reason, Ross had returned to work less than six months later and was promptly sent to Madrid, followed by Washington. And now Cincinnati.

He had never failed, Shelley realized as she read through his accomplishments with Elite. Whatever the situation — incompetent or dishonest management, economic crisis, fierce competition, natural disaster, or sheer apathy — Ross created vibrant success out of failure. In big cities like New York and Tokyo, his success usually had little effect on his competitors, but in smaller cities he efficiently eliminated all competition. He occasionally hired staff from competing schools, thus bankrupting his competitors of employees as well as clients.

Shelley put down the report and tried to calm the panic rising inside her. Ross Tanner could very well destroy her budding career. She knew she was good at her job and believed she could hold her own against stronger competition than Chuck, but it seemed like no one could hold their own against Ross. If she lost everything to Ross, Babel wouldn't simply shrug and offer her another challenging post. Even if they didn't fire her, she would be lucky to find herself cleaning out storage rooms at the distribution center in New Jersey.

She was full of questions. Why had Ross quit, and why had he come back to work? What had he done in the interim? What made him so successful at every aspect of the business? What was his weak spot? He must have one; no one was perfect.

She thought back to the scene in her office earlier that day. Of course he wasn't perfect! He'd been taken in by Chuck, hadn't he? Shelley thought Chuck was quite patently one of the sleaziest men she'd ever met, which was one of the reasons she refused to comply with his pompous request to be called Charles or Mr. Winston-Clarke. If Ross was so clever, why hadn't he figured out immediately that Chuck was a dishonest schmuck dipping his hand into the cookie jar?

Her chief strength in this business was in knowing people. She relied on her intuition, and it had always served her well. If that was the only advantage she had over Ross, she would have to use it cunningly. What's more, she would have to study him. If there was anything about him she could emulate in order to strengthen her position, she would.

Time for bed, she decided. She would need a full night's sleep. In addition to being the director of a business under siege, starting tomorrow she would also be a full-time student. Ross would be her mentor, whether he knew it or not.

*H*e'd acted like a fool. He could see that now, and it bothered him. He was not accustomed to making stupid mistakes. He was disgusted with himself for acting without proper forethought.

Shelley was right, of course. The Elite school was losing money hand over fist, and the financial records were so conveniently messy that no one could trace the loss. The very first thing he should have done was look into Chuck's life-style and expenses. Chuck's insistence that he never touched the financial logbooks and his repeated protests that he didn't understand such things should have merely highlighted his culpability. Ross would definitely have to spend the next couple of days in relentless examination of the accounts for the past few years. Whatever Chuck had done, however well he had hidden it, Ross would figure it out and take the measures necessary to put a stop to it.

Furthermore, Chuck's innuendo about Shelley was such a tired, overused, obvious ploy to cover himself for losing so much business to her that Ross was deeply embarrassed to have fallen for it. Knowing Shelley personally only made him doubly ashamed. And to have gone immediately to her office to confront her about it was so heavy-handed that he could hardly believe he had done it. What the hell was the matter with him lately?

He had let emotion cloud his usually razor-sharp approach. He hadn't wanted to fire Chuck. He was tired of disrupting people's lives, tired of uncomfortable scenes where people begged him for another chance, tired of lowering the boom, even on someone like Chuck who undoubtedly deserved it.

He also realized with wry self-disgust that jealousy had played more than a small part in his behavior. He hadn't wanted to believe or disbelieve Chuck. He had simply wanted to charge into Shelley's office and make sure that no other man had ever touched her before or would ever touch her again. It was ridiculous, of course. She was twenty-eight years old, beautiful, and desirable; naturally other men had touched her and other men would touch her again long after he was gone.

He tried to remember whether he had ever been so irrepressibly jealous before. It wasn't like him. He wasn't possessive and couldn't be possessed. Whatever city he happened to be in, he would meet a woman and, if the chemistry was right, he would become her considerate, carefree, and charming lover with no strings attached.

Nothing like Shelley had ever happened to him before. He was accustomed to being what a woman expected of him: rakish, dashing, slightly mysterious. When the relationship ended, or when he moved on to a new city, he always took care to end the affair with the sort of dramatic flair the woman wanted: a red rose and a tender note; a champagne dinner and a kiss on the hand; an expensive gift and a plea for some memento to remember her by. All tried and true methods — nothing original — but in their own way, good, clean fun that was appreciated yet never taken seriously.

Shelley affected him differently, though, and it bothered him. He supposed that their first meeting did have a certain dramatic flair, but he hadn't planned it and wouldn't have cared if they'd met in a bus station.

Her eyes were always filled with open honesty, candid curiosity, quick perception, and a complete lack of preconceptions. She merely wanted to know what he really was, and she didn't camouflage her true nature in any way. Every time he was with her, he responded physically; he couldn't help it. But he also responded personally, emotionally. He wanted to tell her who he was, what he really thought, how he felt. He enjoyed her reaction to his practiced charm, yet he wanted her to know and accept what lay under the surface. He wanted to make some of her little fantasies come true but, for once, he was aware of fantasies she could fulfill for him, too.

Unfortunately, after yesterday he had a feeling that the only fantasy she cherished about him was seeing the last of him. The report she had about him wouldn't improve matters, either.

He supposed the information had come from Babel's New York and Paris offices. They had made a hobby of checking up on him, particularly since that time in Bangkok when he'd hired away half their staff to fill his own school. He'd heard that the former offices of the Babel school in Bangkok now housed a travel agency.

Of course, a lot of his past was unaccounted for, but he was sure there was enough information to tell Shelley about his wild youth, his wrong-side-of-the-law days, and his ruthless business practices. He wondered which particular aspect of his life would make her loathe him the most.

He glanced at the clock on the wall and realized he'd been daydreaming for quite a while, which also wasn't like him. He would be barely on time for his appointment with Mike Paige at Keene International. It was just after eleven o'clock in the morning, and they had agreed to have lunch together when their meeting was concluded.

Shelley sat in the China Palace, poking at her food and pretending to be enthralled by her companion's conversation. He was Mike Paige's boss, and they had scheduled their meeting to take place in the restaurant. Judging by the man's girth, he undoubtedly scheduled all his meetings in restaurants. Mike did the work of assembling and assessing information about Babel and Elite, but the decision, for some reason, would be left entirely up to his boss. Mike had some influence over him, but probably not enough to ensure Shelley's success. She had a problem on her hands; the man was an insufferable chauvinist and made no secret about his reluctance to do business with a woman. Shelley had been able to win out against Chuck, but now Ross was in town.

"It was a beautiful weapon, but the trigger guard — Do you know anything about shotguns, Michelle?"

"No, I'm afraid not," she admitted. The man was a weapons collector. And a hunter. And a deep-sea fisherman. Apparently if it could kill or be killed, he considered it a good hobby. She loved the China Palace but was losing her appetite after several stories about blowing away little furry creatures with big brown eyes. Where were Mike and Ross? she wondered.

She had called Mike Paige first thing that morning and convinced him to bring Ross to the China Palace after their meeting. They would stop by Shelley's table. Everyone would comment on what a coincidence it was and decide to lunch together. Shelley invented several good reasons for Mike to agree to this plan; her real reason was to study Ross with these potential clients.

"And so was the firing pin," continued her companion, laughing heartily. "Of course, not knowing anything about shotguns or rifles, you couldn't appreciate —"

"What a surprise!" said a smooth voice with just a touch of irony. Shelley turned quickly to find herself staring up into Ross's sparkling blue eyes. Since one glance told her he realized instantly that she'd planned this, she didn't try to pretend otherwise. The slight puzzlement in his eyes told her he just didn't know *why* she had arranged this, and she intended to use that to her advantage.

"Ross! How about this?" exclaimed Mike's boss, obviously thrilled to see a real man's man in their midst. Now was her chance: apart from being male, how would Ross get through to this bloodthirsty lump of flesh who held her future in his paws?

"May we join you?" Ross asked with confident ease.

"By all means! Pull up a chair. I was just telling Michelle here about this guy who tried to sell me . . . Have you two met, by the way?"

"We haven't been formally introduced," Ross said, seating himself next to Shelley and extending his hand.

"That's true," she said laconically. She placed her small hand in his big, warm one. "But I've heard so much about you."

His hand tightened imperceptibly over hers. "Really? And I've heard so little about you. How long have you been in the business?"

Score one, she thought. He'd done it very neatly, too. "Almost two years," she said.

"You've been a director for two years?" he persisted.

She tried unsuccessfully to pull her hand away. "No. I've been a director for one year."

"Ah, I see," he said in a tone that subtly underlined her lack of experience.

Don't get angry, she reminded herself. Simply learn from him. He had just politely and cleverly knocked her down a peg in the client's eyes. It was worth remembering.

He covered their clasped hands with his free hand and used the camouflage to caress her palm with his fingertips. "And how do you like your new job?" he asked charmingly.

"It's hardly new," Shelley said sweetly. "How do you like Cincinnati? Do you find it at all unsettling to do business in a city you can't even find your way around in?"

Ross's eyes danced as she seethed. He quickly squeezed her hand one last time — as if to express appreciation for her riposte — then released it.

"Not at all. What are you eating?"

"Moo Goo Gai Pan."

"*Gesundheit.*"

"That looks good, Shelley," Mike Paige interrupted. "I think that's what I'll have."

"If you can get our waiter back," grumbled Mike's boss. "I haven't seen him for ten minutes. The service here is awful."

Ross looked across the room and said, "Waiter."

Within thirty seconds someone was taking his order, refilling Shelley's water glass, presenting a wine list and clearing away the appetizer plates. She began to suspect that Ross owed his success to a secret ingredient she would never be able to emulate.

While Shelley had planned this luncheon to observe Ross with Mike Paige and his boss, Ross was using the occasion to breach her defenses. He flirted with her outrageously. Mike's boss was too obtuse to notice it. Mike himself was clearly confused, since he knew how fierce the competition between Babel and Elite was for Keene's contract.

Shelley was relieved that Ross had never used the full force of his charm on her when they were alone. She doubted she would have escaped with her sanity intact. He flattered her, he teased her, he listened attentively to every word she uttered, he made her feel beautiful and brilliant and special. And, amazingly, he did this all without ever neglecting their companions. He encouraged Mike and his boss to tell them all about their careers and goals while he burned Shelley's flesh with his hot gaze, warmed her soul with his secretive smiles, confused her with the intensity of his presence.

He was so much more dangerous than she had realized, she thought dazedly. How could she have known, or even guessed? She had never met anyone like him before. He could talk his way into the Kremlin; he could be the first unbeliever allowed inside the Great Mosque at Mecca; he could out-Herod Herod; he could charm the leaves from the trees; he could build the Tower of Babel and get away with it. Even heaven would be taken in by that smile, those eyes, that suggestive voice.

Stop it, Shelley, stop it, she chided herself. She knew full well what he was doing, and she was still overwhelmed. She had always detested flirts, always been suspicious of easy charm, and yet he had her eating out of his hand. Time to take charge, she decided.

She stiffened her spine and shifted her body away from Ross. Everyone's attitude indicated that it would be gauche to bring up business now or press Keene for a decision. The next best thing would be to take everyone's attention off Ross. With wide, enraptured eyes she questioned Mike's boss about his loathsome hobbies.

"The biggest set of antlers I've ever seen. . . ." the man was saying ten minutes later as the plates were cleared away. Every time there was a pause in the conversation she shifted attention back to him, willfully keeping Ross from making any further impression on the group.

Ross sat back with an amused expression and made no attempt to interfere. She wanted to snap at him that she hadn't planned this meeting for his personal pleasure, but knew it would only increase his enjoyment.

"There's this place in Pennsylvania . . ."

Shelley sipped her coffee, letting her hand drop down to dangle beside her chair. Within seconds she felt warm, strong fingers stroke her palm and then interlace with her own fingers.

She drew in her breath sharply, drawing Mike's gaze. "How exciting," she murmured. She saw Ross's grin out of the corner of her eye and wished she had chosen different words.

"It was an antique, genuine eighteenth century. Worth thousands . . ."

Shelley tried to pull her hand away and Ross's grip tightened. Slowly, inexorably, he pulled her hand closer to him as he shifted his body towards her. There was a predatory glitter in his hooded eyes that made her heart beat faster. His free hand covered hers, and he began to gently massage the soft underside of her wrist.

Shelley's lips parted and she felt her breath grow shallow. She kept her eyes firmly fixed on their companions and wondered what she would do about this. Those strong caressing fingers sent little hot waves of pleasure running up her arm and into her chest.

He gently, caressingly squeezed her wrist, relaxed and squeezed again and again and again, establishing an unmistakable, suggestive rhythm. As soon as the thought flashed into her mind, she felt her cheeks flush. She would kill him for this. As if taking pity on her crumbling composure, he ceased his teasing massage to trail his fingers back down her wrist with a feather-light touch and tickle her palm.

The sensation nearly forced a throaty sigh from her. She bit back the noise with effort, and, as a result, her teeth chattered. That drew a surprised and laughing glance from Ross.

"Are you cold, Shelley?" he asked with insufferable concern.

"No," she said tersely.

"You look kind of hot, actually," Mike interjected. "You're all flushed."

"Really?" she said weakly.

"Your eyes are glittering, too," said Ross with exaggerated seriousness. "Perhaps you have a fever." He maintained his grasp on her hand while his free hand came out from under the table and reached for her brow.

"Of course, I don't —"

"Shh, talking raises your temperature," he crooned while he felt her forehead, touched her cheek, rubbed the back of her neck, and stroked the soft skin under her chin.

"That's ridiculous," she snapped, trying to pull away from his blatantly intimate touch.

"There's a lot of flu going around," Mike suggested.

"Excuse me, sir, here's your bill," said a waiter.

Mike and his boss turned away from Shelley and started arguing about which of them would put the lunch on his expense account. Shelley was about to enter into the argument, but Ross distracted her.

"Do you think you might swoon?" he inquired solicitously.

"That does it," she muttered, "I really *am* going to kill you for this."

"But Shelley, dear, this lunch was your idea," he pointed out wickedly.

"Not all of it," she said, and yanked her hand forcefully out of his. She turned her attention to the men from Keene International. "Please, I insist you let me pick up the check."

Both men argued with that, Mike out of courtesy and the other man because Shelley was a mere woman. Ross sat back and let them all bicker about who would pay for lunch. Shelley finally agreed to let Mike's boss pay, realizing it was the silly sort of thing that would confirm his manliness to himself.

"Did you bring a coat?" Ross asked Shelley as they approached the exit.

"Yes, it's right in here." She walked into the cloakroom and found her simple beige blazer. Just as she was about to pull it off the hanger, Ross appeared next to her and removed it for her. With that curiously old-fashioned courtesy she had seen in him before, he helped her put it on. Then he ruined the effect by suggestively stroking her arm and grinning with pleasure at her exasperation.

Mike's boss preceded them out of the restaurant, and despite the man's vocal views on the defenseless sex, he let the door swing back in Shelley's face. Mike rolled his eyes apologetically. Ross opened the door and ushered Shelley out into the breezy April afternoon on Sixth Street.

After exchanging the usual courtesies, Mike Paige asked, "How are you getting back, Shelley?"

"We'll walk. It's not far," Ross said.

"We?" Shelley said apprehensively.

"I'm going your way," he replied.

"But Elite isn't —"

"My father taught me to always see a lady to her door."

"But I —"

"Good, good, we won't have to worry about her now," said Mike's boss, probably thinking what a *man* Ross was. Shelley bit back a snarl of irritation. "We'll be talking to you, Ross . . . and to you, too, Michelle. Goodbye."

Mike Paige nodded weakly to Shelley and Ross, and the two men climbed into a taxi. Mike's boss obviously found walking four blocks back to work too strenuous.

"So much for the great white hunter," Shelley murmured.

"That was fun, wasn't it?" Ross said cheerfully. "We must do this more often, Shelley."

Shelley whirled on him. Her mouth worked, but no sound came out.

"You look quite overwhelmed, Shelley. I sometimes have that effect on women," he confided, "but you'll get over it when you get more accustomed to me."

"I have no intention of getting accustomed to you! And as soon as I can think of something cutting and rude enough to say to you, I —"

"Temper, temper. I was just trying to lighten the atmosphere at lunch. All those stories about slaughtering Bambi seemed to be spoiling your appetite."

She pursed her lips for a moment and then, quite against her will, started to laugh. Ross smiled appreciatively.

"There, that's better. I like to see you laugh," he said, tilting his head to one side. His eyes raked her severe brown skirt and beige top. "It makes you look more like yourself."

She sighed, wishing she could feel angry or order him to leave her alone. With a warm feeling of inevitability, she turned and started walking up the street, knowing he would tag along and feeling glad for it.

"I don't suppose you'd care to tell me why you orchestrated this chance meeting today?" he asked conversationally.

"I don't suppose you'd like to tell me what you offered Keene International today?" she countered.

"I don't mind. I imagine Mike Paige will tell you soon enough, anyhow."

She looked at Ross in surprise. It hadn't occurred to her that he would actually answer her question.

"Well?" she prompted.

He looked at her consideringly for a moment, and she had a sense again of the shrewdness he brought to his work.

Most of the time, she amended silently, remembering their scene in her office.

"I offered the usual native speakers, bonus lessons, inclusive materials, certified interpreters and so on. I offered to send the instructors to Keene's offices at no extra charge; Elite will pick up the travel expenses."

Shelley frowned, thinking. She could certainly match that offer, although it would take some bargaining with her superiors to get them to cover travel expenses for instructors and interpreters. "What else?"

"Free limousine service, complimentary hotel suite for visiting foreigners, Elite buys meals for all private intensive students."

"Is there more?" she asked apprehensively.

There certainly was. Ross outlined schedules and services Shelley couldn't provide at prices she couldn't match.

"You can't make a profit on that deal," she said skeptically when he had finished. "Will Elite let you do that?" She frowned again and looked away. "Of course they will," she murmured, "with your record. You must have done this before."

He glanced at her. "I take it you've read all about me?"

"Yes," she answered pensively.

"And?"

"And I think you're very clever." She looked away again. "That's your plan for Cincinnati, isn't it? Elite's reputation is so bad here you need a big client like Keene to sign with you no matter what it costs you. They'll give you the credibility you need to attract everyone else's business, which you'll charge normal prices for. Next year, when you renew Keene's contract you'll charge them enough to break even. Two years from now you'll charge enough to make a handsome profit off them. But by then you'll be firmly entrenched and growing rich off everybody."

He was silent for a moment. The breeze stirred his black hair, tumbling it over his forehead. "You're very quick, Shelley," he said at last.

"Does Mike Paige know?"

"I don't think he knows yet. He'll figure it out eventually. But it won't matter."

"No, it won't, will it? Because whatever your motive, you're offering him more than I can at a better price."

"Exactly." His voice was soft, filled with something that she might have mistaken for regret.

"So it won't even matter that Chuck is still your director. They'll want to do business with you anyhow."

"Chuck won't be in charge anymore, Shelley."

She looked at him with obvious surprise. He stopped and turned toward her. He took her arm and drew her under the wide stone stairway leading up to the skywalk. In the soft shadows, with his rich blue eyes and with the wind touching his raven hair, he looked like one of her more intense fantasies come to lure her away from her responsible job and her practical nature.

"You're getting rid of Chuck?" she asked weakly. He nodded. "Why?"

"Because he's dishonest, fraudulent, incompetent and incapable." He sighed. "I'm so tired of taking away people's jobs. I didn't want to do it again."

"But it's for the best, Ross," Shelley said softly, only vaguely aware that it was absurd to think about comforting him.

"I know." His warm hand came up to stroke her face. "He doesn't know yet. I'm trusting you with a secret."

"I won't say anything."

"I believe you." He pushed a copper-colored strand of hair away from her face and tucked it behind her ear in, a peculiarly tender gesture. He caressed her thick ponytail tumbling wildly behind her head. "I love your hair," he murmured. "It looks like you just got out of bed."

"Thanks a lot," she said dryly.

"I didn't mean it that way. It makes you look soft," he murmured. "Touchable." His gaze shifted to her mouth. "Sexy." His eyes half closed, hiding his expression, but not before she'd seen the sudden flash of desire there. It pierced through her, tugging at her own needs. In the few days since they'd met, had she known a single moment when he wasn't in her thoughts?

"Ross . . ." She had meant to sound matter-of-fact, but she practically purred his name.

"I'm sorry about yesterday," he whispered. His fingers traced the line of her collar. "I lost my head. I was sitting there thinking about what an honest person you were, then Chuck told me . . . I don't know . . . I just couldn't stand the thought of anyone else touching you."

She heard the confusion in his low voice, the possessiveness, and wondered at it. "I haven't got the basic equipment to be a scarlet woman," she said breathlessly.

"Oh, Shelley," he sighed affectionately. "What a lot you have to learn."

His mouth captured hers — warm, pliant, coaxing — gently but relentlessly demanding. They slid naturally into each other's arms as his lips begged a response from hers. The past hour, she realized suddenly, had been nothing but foreplay, all thrust and parry, hide and seek. She could have cut him short at any point during lunch, but she had let him see her interest, her excitement.

He pulled back and kissed her again and again, nibbling at her lips, nuzzling her throat, increasing his demands. She sensed he was seeking something special from her, something he couldn't put a name to. She opened herself to him willingly, wanting to give him whatever he needed from her. She hid nothing, denied him nothing, and demanded the same commitment from him as their mouths slanted hungrily across each other.

He pulled away quite suddenly. His breath was shallow and rapid. His hand came up to her jaw and he studied her with an intense, confused frown, as if she had done something outside his experience.

"What is it?" she asked huskily, watching him with candid vulnerability.

"You . . ." He kissed her lightly again, with shattering tenderness, then released her.

She gazed at him, sensing another struggle going on inside him that she was sure involved more than desire. Something had cracked his smooth exterior, and he was wary and surprised.

She took a deep breath and realized that it was just as well that something had abruptly interrupted their mutual fascination. This was hardly the place.

"I have to get back to work," she said inanely.

"Of course." He willfully forced the surprised confusion out of his expression and regained his usual composure. Shelley suddenly wondered how much else he kept hidden under that debonair manner and easy charm. She thought back to what she'd read about his chaotic youth, his wild escapades, his rebellious life. He was much more complicated than she had suspected.

"You're a slippery character," she murmured pensively.

He grinned at that. He took her hand and kissed it with excessive gallantry. "Indeed I am. But you're a tough woman. I imagine you could kick me into shape."

She shook her head in amusement. "I'm a busy woman," she corrected. She sobered as he led her out of the shadow of the stairs. "I have to call my boss in Chicago, Ross. I have to tell him what you're planning. I have to."

His own humor fled at once. "I know."

"I . . . don't want you to walk me the rest of the way back to work."

He nodded, seemingly lost in thought. Just before he turned away from her he said, "Will I see you again this week?"

She hesitated for a long moment before saying, "I don't think so, Ross."

"Shelley, we need —"

"Please, don't say any more. I just don't know what to do. I'm under pressure from everyone right now. Don't add to it," she pleaded.

She thought he would argue and was perversely disappointed when he agreed to respect her wishes. She turned to leave and, after she'd taken a few steps, heard him call her name. Heart pounding, she looked over her shoulder.

"Yes?"

His eyes were dancing again, as they had at lunch, and she knew he was up to something. "Still looking for a Pashto interpreter?"

"How did you — Oh." She remembered he'd been in her lobby yesterday to witness her disappointment. "I'm still looking," she admitted.

"Well, if you don't find anyone, I know one."

"You do? Who? Where?" she asked eagerly, taking a few steps toward him.

"Oh, no," he chided. "I want you to come to me for it. And when you do, I'll want something in return."

He actually had the gall to wink at her. He sauntered away jauntily, leaving her to stare after him in exasperation.

Five

"You know," Shelley said to Wayne three days later, "bureaucracy is a remarkable thing. I've made numerous phone calls, sent a detailed written report and offered a dozen specific suggestions about our situation here. And the great minds at headquarters have brilliantly deduced that Ross Tanner may try to get a contract with Keene International and that I have to stop him."

"That's all?" Wayne asked.

"That's all. They haven't given me any more bargaining tools, any more independent authority, or even any more money for business lunches. How do they expect me to get that contract?" she said in frustration.

"Proposition Mike Paige," Wayne offered.

"That is a vulgar suggestion," Francesca said as she set down a tray of coffee on Shelley's desk.

"Call Jerome in Chicago," Wayne amended meekly.

"I did. He promised to talk to them personally and explain everything in words of one syllable." She crumpled a piece of paper and threw it in the trashcan across the room.

"They even denied the pay raise I requested for Ute. You know, sometimes I feel like they're the bad guys. I mean, how am I supposed to run a good business with them getting in my way all the time?"

"My father worked for the Italian government when I was a *bambina*, and things like this used to happen to him all the time," Francesca said.

"Really? What did he do?" Wayne asked thoughtfully.

"He ignored their instructions and did what he knew had to be done."

"This isn't Calabria, Francesca. They'd find out immediately and they'd fire me on the spot." Shelley sipped her coffee. "Despite everything, I still like my job and I don't want to go looking for another one."

"Perhaps you can convince Ross Tanner to let you have this one contract," Francesca suggested.

"How?"

Wayne looked at Francesca. Francesca looked at Shelley. Shelley looked blank.

"He is very attracted to you," Francesca said slyly.

"Hey . . ." Wayne said slowly. "Maybe —"

"Absolutely not!" Shelley interrupted. "How could you even suggest such a thing? You're starting to sound like Chuck."

"I did not mean anything improper, Shelley," Francesca said placatingly. "A simple request made at a moment when he's feeling gallant and generous."

"Yeah," said Wayne.

"Shelley, *cara*, he could hardly take his eyes off you when he was here."

"Yeah," said Wayne.

"Perhaps you could influence him —"

"Yeah!" Wayne obviously loved this plan.

"Forget it," Shelley said firmly. "Apart from the fact that he's a very clever, experienced and ruthless man, how could you suggest I compromise my self-respect that way? Then I really would be no more than what Chuck implied."

"Americans," Francesca sighed. She shrugged and left the room.

The telephone rang. Eager to change the subject, Shelley picked it up immediately. "Babel Language Center. Can I help you?"

"Shelley, have you found a Pashto interpreter yet?"

Shelley gave a deep sigh. It was the interpreters' coordinator in Washington. "No, I haven't."

The woman's vituperative response was so loud that Shelley had to hold the phone away from her ear. Wayne's eyes widened and he huddled in his chair.

"Yes, I know there's so little time left." Shelley closed her eyes as another loud wave of angry criticism washed over her. "Calm down, calm down. I have a very good lead. I'm checking into it today. I'll call you first thing Monday morning, okay?" She slammed down the receiver before the angry woman could exercise her vocal chords again.

"Do you really have a good lead?" Wayne asked cautiously.

"Yes, I do," Shelley said resignedly. "I'm going to go see about it right now."

Shelley put on a gray blazer and left Babel. As she walked over to Elite, she reflected on the irony of her situation. The one man who was out to hurt her most was also the only man who could help her in this case.

Her plan to learn how he did business hadn't gone as she had intended, but she had at least seen the effect he had on business associates and had deduced his strategy for rebuilding Elite's reputation and business in Cincinnati.

What's more, wrapped in his arms, enthralled by his dizzying kisses, she had discovered an unexpected level of vulnerability in him that she intuitively knew few people ever got to see. The discovery made him all the more appealing, all the more fascinating to her. However, if it was intriguing to know he was vulnerable, it was also unsettling to know he could hide it so well. He was even more dangerous to her now. And since her staff had just blithely urged her to encourage his attentions in order to secure her company's success against him, Shelley knew his presence could be embarrassing to her, as well.

She felt so confused that she almost wished he would go away before it was too late. Too late for what, she wasn't yet sure. She only knew that nothing in her life had prepared her for Ross, while everything in her life had trained her to be loyal to her employer, her employees, her clients, and her sense of what was right. And the strange, unsettling rightness of being with Ross disturbed all her notions of where her loyalties lay.

She pushed open the heavy glass door to Elite's lobby and stopped in surprise. There were half a dozen workmen inside, stripping wallpaper, ripping out the light fixtures, hauling away old furniture, and generally wreaking havoc. Shelley felt glum. She had been trying to get money to redecorate for nearly a year, while Ross had achieved this goal in just one week.

She felt momentarily surprised to realize that it had only been one week since that fateful moment when she'd spotted him across a crowded room. So much had happened since then, it was hard to believe he'd only been disrupting her life for a handful of days. Would it all have turned out differently, she wondered, if she hadn't had a moment alone with him before finding out who he was? She shrugged. Perhaps they'd never share any level of intimacy, but she would still be drawn to him; there was no point in pretending otherwise.

She looked around for the receptionist. There was no sign of the woman, and Shelley realized she was probably at lunch. Would Ross also be at lunch? Perhaps she should have called ahead.

"What are *you* doing here?" said a thin voice behind her.

Shelley whirled and found herself facing Chuck. They hadn't actually spoken face-to-face since the day she'd sworn out the peace bond, and she had no desire to speak to him now.

"I'm here to see Ross," she replied coolly.

Chuck looked livid. "You're too late. I've already resigned, so you can forget about telling him any more lies."

Shelley ignored that. "This doesn't concern you. Where is he?"

"Are you after my job?"

"If you've just resigned, it's not your job anymore, is it? Is he in?"

"You've wanted to get rid of me from the first, haven't you?" Chuck said in a low, accusing voice.

"I've wanted to run my business professionally," she corrected. "You haven't answered my question. Is he here?"

"He won't pay any more attention to you than I did. You and your tight skirts and your —"

"That's quite enough, Chuck," Shelley interrupted sharply, masking her surprise as well as she could.

"Going around looking like —"

"The lady said that's quite enough, Charles." It was Ross's cool, authoritative voice.

Shelley looked up in surprise to see him standing in a shadowed doorway just down the hall. Relief washed through her. Chuck had been about to make a nasty scene, the general tone of which would have been as disgusting as it was unexpected.

"Shelley, what a pleasant surprise," Ross said cheerfully, trying to banish the tension among the three of them. "Please come in and have a seat." He ushered Shelley into his office and glanced briefly at Chuck. "Nearly through gathering your belongings, Charles?"

The meekness of Chuck's muffled reply relieved Shelley. She was glad Ross could handle him in this mood, since it frightened her a little bit.

She had guessed how intensely Chuck hated her, but he had always tried to keep it hidden until now. She suddenly realized how glad she was to know she would never have to deal with him again.

"Have a seat," Ross invited. "I'm afraid it's a little cramped in here."

"Why are you in this tiny room? The director's office is beautiful, if I remember correctly."

"I'm not the director," he reminded her.

"Neither is Chuck, I gather. He said he's resigned. You gave him the chance to, rather than fire him, didn't you?"

"It was the best alternative, for both him and the company."

"And for you?"

He hesitated a moment, and she sensed he felt uncomfortable about having revealed that vulnerability to her. "It was the best choice for me, too," he admitted.

"So who will sit in that office now?"

"Whoever I decide to hire." His eyes avoided hers. "I just sort out the mess and put things in order. I never stay."

"Yes. I'd forgotten." There was an uncomfortable silence. "So you're looking for a new director?"

"I may have found someone."

"So fast?"

"I'm not sure yet."

"Anyone I know?" she prodded.

He smiled charmingly and changed the subject. "What brings you here today? Dare I hope you couldn't stay away from me any longer?"

Shelley rolled her eyes. "Actually, I can't stay away from your Pashto interpreter any longer."

"Ahh, the job is coming up soon, is it?"

"Yes, it's next week, and none of my contacts can find anyone acceptable. If you really can help me with this, Ross, I'd be so grateful I'd . . .I'd . . .I'd be very grateful," she finished lamely.

He grinned, and she knew he was going to toy with her just a little bit for making him wait so long.

"So, you need something only I can provide," he said musingly.

"You did offer," she reminded him.

"I seem to recall saying I'd want something in return," he murmured.

"Did you?" she hedged.

"Oh, yes. I never do anything for free."

"I gathered that."

"Yes, you've read all about me, haven't you?"

"What could I possibly offer you, Mr. Tanner, that you don't already have or can't get without my help?" she asked dryly.

His eyes raked her slowly, so thoroughly that she wondered whether all her buttons were done up. "A number of things come to mind," he said suggestively, "and I suspect some of them would make your father want to shoot me."

Shelley shifted uncomfortably. She reminded herself that he was a heartless flirt and a sophisticated charmer, but she couldn't control the sudden flutter of her heart or the warm feeling that started pulsing deep inside her belly.

"I suppose a dirty weekend is out of the question?" he asked.

Shelley laughed. "I like it when you're gauche."

He sighed. "Then I suppose I'll have to settle for lunch. Your timing's perfect, in fact. I was just getting hungry."

"Wait a minute," she said as he reached for his jacket. "Take care of my problem first, and then we'll talk about lunch. Who's this interpreter you're going to get for me?"

"He's an old friend of mine. We go way back."

"Are you positive he can do the job? It requires a very sophisticated level —"

"He's a professor of English literature, Shelley, so I think it's safe to say he's up to the job. He's also a U.S. citizen now. I asked."

"You asked? When did you ask?"

"A few days ago. I figured you'd need him. I told him to be ready to come to Cincinnati. I'll have him call you this afternoon to make arrangements."

"Where is he?"

"Berkeley."

"California?"

"Yes. Can we go eat now? I'm starving," he complained, shrugging into his jacket.

"Wait a minute, wait a minute! He's coming here from California?"

"That's what I just said, Shelley. Come on, stand up. Please don't tell me you're in the mood for Chinese again."

"Who's paying for it?" she demanded.

"My treat, I insist. Just don't —"

"No," she interrupted irritably, "who's paying for your friend's flight out here?"

"He is, I imagine. Unless he's got an exceptionally rich and generous girlfriend these days. How does Italian strike you? Or maybe French?" He took her hand and started pulling her down the hallway, past the confusion in the lobby.

"Hey, Mr. Tanner," said a workman. "Do you want to keep these chairs?"

"Good Lord, no. They look like they were bought at a garage sale."

"You want we should throw them out?" the man asked.

"Yes, please do."

"Ross! Why is he doing this?"

"He can't throw things out without asking first," Ross explained patiently.

"You know what I mean! Why is your friend — ?"

"Oh, him. He owes me a favor."

"It must have been a pretty big favor."

"It was. I wonder if we can get a table at the Maisonette at this time of day," he mused, propelling her out the door.

"Ross!" Shelley yanked her arm out of his hand. "I . . . You . . . Why are you doing this?"

"Because I'm hungry."

She gritted her teeth in exasperation. "Why are you doing this for me?" she demanded.

He smiled whimsically. "Let's discuss it over lunch, shall we?"

*T*he Maisonette was the best restaurant in Cincinnati. It was probably also the most expensive, which was why Shelley had never eaten there. Judging by the friendly greeting they got at the door and the way a table was quickly procured for them, Shelley guessed that Ross had already become a regular client there. Her suspicions were confirmed when the headwaiter addressed Ross by name.

The two men chatted in French for a few moments, Ross assuring him that the table was perfectly acceptable, particularly since he hadn't reserved in advance. Then the waiter turned to Shelley and apologized in English for using a language she couldn't understand.

"Mais ça ne fait rien. Elle parle français," Ross said and looked at Shelley for verification. *"C'est vrai que to le parle, n'est-ce pas?"*

"Oui, mais comment est-ce que tu le savais?" Shelley asked, wondering for the first time whether there was a report about her sitting on Ross's desk.

"Chuck told me you'd been a language major at college," Ross explained. "I just assumed you'd speak it."

Ross exhibited those endearingly old-fashioned manners again when he ordered her food, acting as liaison between herself and the waiter. It was on the tip of her tongue to say it was silly for him to ask her what she wanted and then repeat it to the waiter as if she couldn't speak for herself, but he did it with such a delicate touch of gallantry that she didn't have the heart to spoil the scene.

When they were alone again, sipping their fabulous French wine and awaiting their first course, she said, "I've always wanted to come here. This hardly seems like I'm making fair payment for the favor you're doing me."

"Perhaps I should make you pay for it," he suggested evilly.

"Too late. I can't afford it." She tilted her head thoughtfully. "But I suppose you can. Henri Montpazier must pay you a lot to go around the world resuscitating his business empire."

"He does. He pays according to merit rather than according to a fixed scale."

She sighed, the wine loosening her up a bit. "I wish Babel did. They're so inflexible about pay scales."

He studied her thoughtfully as their appetizers were put before them.

Shelley looked down at her *pâté de venaison chaude en sauce poivrade.* "I think I've died and gone to heaven," she murmured.

Ross grinned, enjoying her pleasure. "Don't gobble," he chided.

"Oh, gosh, this is good. I've never tasted anything so good," she said in ecstasy.

"Can I have a taste?"

"Not on your life," she said, shoving his hand away as he moved his fork toward her plate.

"I had no idea you were so greedy."

"I had no idea food could be like this. What are you eating?" she asked.

"*Salmis de faisan en caneton en feuilleté avec sauce aux truffes.*"

"Gosh, that sounds good."

"It's just chicken potpie, only with pheasant and duck," he replied.

"What a snob you are. Give me a bite." She reached across the table and took a forkful from him.

"Wait a minute," he said in amusement. "Why can you eat mine but I can't eat yours?"

"Because you get to come here all the time, and I never will again."

"You could come here more often," he said persuasively.

"With you?" she asked suspiciously.

He smiled lazily. "That's one possibility."

"Oh, yeah? What's the other?"

He leaned back in his chair and looked at her silently for a moment, a subtle smile playing around his mouth as he watched her devour both their appetizers.

"If you think watching me eat will make me shy, you're dead wrong," she informed him. "In my family, you learned to dive in or go hungry."

"You had a big family?"

She nodded and reached for more of his food. "I was the fourth of five girls."

He raised his brows. "Did you all go to college?"

"Oh, yes. On scholarships and loans, mostly. I'm still paying mine back. My parents were very big on education. They weren't able to go to college themselves, and they wanted us all to get a good education, good jobs and financial security."

"And were their plans realized?"

"Well . . . one of my sisters wants to be an actress, so she lives like a church mouse, and my oldest sister is some sort of left-wing journalist in California. But the other two make good money. Aren't you going to eat any of this?"

"In a minute."

"There won't be any left in a minute," she warned him, taking another bite.

"What about you? Are you satisfied with your salary?" he prodded.

Shelley frowned. "I'm not sure I want to talk about this with you."

"Actually, Shelley, I already know what you make. And it's not nearly what you deserve."

She looked at him in surprise. "How do you know my salary?"

"I have my sources," he replied blandly.

She shrugged after a moment. "Well, I suppose it's hardly top secret. And I *do* deserve more."

"You can have more, Shelley. I . . . *We* can offer you double what you make now. Plus an expense account, four weeks paid vacation and full benefits. And that's just to start with."

Shelley put down her fork and stared at Ross in stunned silence. Her gray eyes grew round. Finally she whispered, "What?"

"I told you I'm looking for a new director for the language center. I want the most qualified, capable person I can find," he said. "That's you, Shelley."

Shock reeled through her, dulling her wits and stilling her tongue. She had always thought of Elite as her nemesis at best, and as a thoroughly unprofessional operation at worst.

The possibility of working for them had never even entered her mind.

"You want me . . ." She shook her head in confusion.

"Listen," Ross insisted. His blue eyes were businesslike, his manner calm and professional. "I have the authority to hire anyone I choose to for any position I deem fit. What's more, I've spoken to Henri about you, and he's already agreed upon the increased salary and benefits I'm offering you."

"You've told him about this?" she said in breathless wonder. "You really do work fast."

"Babel isn't paying you nearly what you deserve, your hands are tied by an inefficient bureaucracy —"

"Elite is just as big as Babel, maybe bigger. Surely you must have bureaucratic confusion, too, otherwise Chuck wouldn't have gotten away with so much all this time."

"We have the same problems, but you won't have to worry about them."

"Why not?" she challenged.

"Because I'll be here, and I have a free hand. I don't have to okay anything with headquarters."

"And when you go?"

"You'll still have me. I'll be your direct contact when you need to clear something. I can also arrange for you to have a lot more independent authority than you have now."

Shelley looked at him helplessly, irresistibly drawn to his offer but totally confused. "But why?"

"Because you're very good at your job, Shelley. In one year you've increased Babel's business in Cincinnati by more than thirty percent. You have an excellent reputation throughout the city. Mike Paige is so impressed with you that even my offer hasn't swayed him in his desire to sign a contract with you. I've seen you with your students and staff. I've seen you with clients. I've seen you in the midst of chaos in your office. And I've always been impressed."

Shelley gazed at him, undeniably pleased with his approbation, proud that someone as successful as Ross admired her ability and had faith in her potential. Offering her double her current salary was certainly a firm expression of that faith. She pushed her plate away and sat back in her chair, trying to organize her thoughts.

"Wow," she said inanely.

"I realize this has come as a surprise to you."

"*That's* an understatement."

"I assure you the offer is genuine and that I've thought it over thoroughly."

"What about Babel?"

"Resign. Two weeks' notice should be sufficient. It's all they deserve."

"Resign?" she asked weakly. "But I . . . I can't just walk over to Elite and start doing business there."

"Why not?"

"Well, I . . . What about my responsibilities at Babel?"

"They'll be taken over by the new director," he said reasonably. "Elite will be your responsibility from now on."

"But what about . . . Wayne and Francesca? What about Ute and Hiroko and Sasha? What about Pablo Gutierrez? I promised him I wouldn't let them kick him out of the country."

"Shelley —"

"I *promised* him, Ross. And then there's Mr. Powell. He'll never learn another language if I'm not there to be firm with him. And there's that girl trying to learn French so she can talk to her new mother-in-law. She always needs me to . . . Ross, I can't just drop all that and move over to Elite."

"Perhaps in time those teachers and clients will also —"

"Clients! My God, what will they say, all my clients? After the way

I've convinced them all that Babel is the best place in town. What will they think when I suddenly turn around and start saying that I was wrong before and Elite is really the best?"

"They'll realize —"

"Realize what? That I've been bought? That I have no integrity?"

"Of course not."

"And what will Elite's staff think? After all the business I've taken from them, they must hate me."

"They don't hate you. I'm sure they don't."

"What do you know about it? If Chuck could fool you, anybody could!"

"He didn't exactly . . . Well . . ."

"And Babel, what will they say? They'll blacken my name in every city around the globe."

"I think that's a slight exaggeration."

"They gave me a job, trained me, gave me this post —"

"And they pay you inadequately to work long hours while they leave you understaffed and don't support you against your competition —"

"Oh, yeah? Well, all that will change soon."

"When?" he challenged.

"When I get this contract with Keene. That's when I'll get my promotion, my raise, more office staff . . ." She stopped abruptly and stared at him with growing despair. "Oh, no."

"Shelley, you don't have to hang on to a hopeless wish to get what you deserve. This is a simple business decision, a fair and honest offer made by a company that has the sense to recognize and reward your worth."

"My worth? What would I be worth if I simply bounced from Babel to Elite like that? Even my mother would be disappointed in me."

"If we're taking personal matters into account here, I think you should consider me, too."

"You? What about you?"

His eyes softened and his expression became intimate. "I'm offering you the job because you're the best choice, and I don't agree with the obstacles you're worried about. But I would also like to point out that if you took it, we would no longer be competitors. We'd be colleagues, working together."

"And you think we'd be unbeatable," she said stiffly.

"I think we'd be inseparable," he said meaningfully.

She nearly forgot to breathe as she drowned in the depths of Ross's gaze, thinking of the two of them together, day after day, building a business, building a relationship. . . .

"Inseparable?" she said. "Until you go away again. And then what?"

He frowned and looked away from her. "We'll work something out."

"Oh, you'll keep in touch," she said sarcastically. "From where? Bangkok? Marrakech? Paris?"

"Let's cross that bridge when we come to it," he said evasively.

She was ashamed she'd believed the sincerity in his eyes for even a moment, embarrassed that she'd even briefly pictured the two of them working side by side, sharing triumphs and confidences in some idyllic work-and-play relationship. He must have proposed this a dozen times before. It must be one of his oldest tricks. Well, it wouldn't work with her.

"Forget it," she said flatly. "Forget the whole thing. I do not want to be your protégée or your paramour, and I will not let you ruin my career —"

"*Ruin* your career? I'm trying to help it!"

"Or ruin my reputation or my self-respect. I should have realized that this friendly invitation to lunch, like every other gesture you've ever made, had an ulterior motive. I was right the first time — you're a very slippery character."

"Will you please try to think objectively?"

"My entire career could depend on this contract with Keene. I had it in the bag until you showed up! I don't care what it takes, but I won't let you ruin this for me, either." She lowered her voice when she noticed several people nearby starting to stare.

Ross made a visible effort to regain his usual calm. "All right," he said after a moment. "You don't want the job. I'd like you to think about it for a while, but," he added as she started to interrupt, "I won't press the issue. In the meantime why don't we try to enjoy the rest of our meal?"

Shelley stared glumly at her plate. "I'm not hungry anymore."

He sighed and leaned back. "Frankly, neither am I."

"Do you think they have doggy bags here?"

Ross smiled in genuine amusement. "I doubt it."

"I think I'd like to go back to work now."

"Yes, maybe we'd better." Ross paid the check, assuring their waiter that there was nothing wrong with the meal. "Miss Baird has just suddenly remembered a pressing appointment with her reflexologist," he explained.

"I see," said the waiter, clearly reassessing Shelley.

"You're incorrigible," she chided Ross as they left the restaurant.

"I've been told that before. On a number of occasions."

"Yes. I know."

"I can see it'll be impossible to be a man of mystery around you. You seem to know every detail of my wicked, wicked past."

"No, just the generalities. The details were missing. But I'm dying to know if it's all true."

His lips twitched. "More true than I care to admit." They reached a street corner. "Well, here's where we part, though not for long, I hope."

"Don't get those hopes up," she advised him. Then she added hesitantly, "I suppose you want your Pashto interpreter back."

"No. Keep him as a gesture of good faith. No strings attached."

"I don't believe that for a moment."

"You wound me. Oh, wait a minute. I almost forgot. Here." He handed her a small printed card. It was an invitation. "We're having an open house at Elite next week. I hope you'll come. Of course, I'd been hoping to introduce you to everyone as our new —"

"Don't push it, Ross."

He shrugged. "Oh, well. I hope you'll come, anyhow"

"I don't think I'd feel comfortable."

"Of course you will. You'll know lots of people there."

"Lots of . . . You're inviting my clients, too, aren't you?"

He nodded.

"Oh, Ross, of all the language schools, in all the towns, in all the world, you walk into this one."

He frowned. "Funny. I think I've heard that before somewhere."

Six

Shelley held the telephone away from her ear as a string of sordid invective burst forth from the receiver. She smiled with smug satisfaction, blissfully aware that she was about to douse the fire.

"Are you still there?" she said loudly into the receiver. "Okay, okay, calm down. I was just kidding."

The voice from the receiver sharply questioned Shelley's legitimacy, breeding, and species. It was amazing how stress affected some people.

"Yes. I've found a Pashto interpreter," Shelley said cheerfully into the receiver.

"You've found someone? You've *found* someone! Oh, my God! Who? Where? When? How?" cried the relieved interpreters' coordinator in Washington.

"He's a native of Afghanistan, a professor of English literature, and an American citizen." She didn't add that he also looked like a desert prince from an old Technicolor movie. Sloe-eyed, bronze-skinned and rather intimidating, Ross's Afghan friend, who preferred to be called Tim, sat in Shelley's office with regal bearing this cheery Monday morning.

"And you're sure he's going to do the job?" prodded the woman on the phone. "We've got less than twenty-four hours left, Shelley. I don't have to tell you —"

"No, you certainly don't. May I remind you that this is not the first time I've arranged a local interpreter for your contracts with the feds in this region," Shelley said with dignity.

"No. No, I realize that." The woman actually sounded slightly cowed.

"We're finishing up the final paperwork now. I anticipate no difficulties and can assure you that everything will go smoothly at this end."

"Good. Thank you," the woman said at last. "And . . . Shelley?"

"Yes?"

"Those things I said earlier? I didn't mean them personally."

"No, of course not," said Shelley blandly, her ears still ringing.

She replaced the receiver in its cradle with an amused smile and turned her attention to Tim. His dark eyes shone with similar amusement. "You have a wicked sense of humor," he said. "Like Ross."

"Only when I'm provoked," she replied. "Do you have any further questions about the job?"

"No. You've explained everything with admirable precision," he said gallantly.

"Thank you. And thank you for coming so far to do this little two-day job for me. The interpretation fee won't even cover your expenses. How can I ever repay you?"

"There is no need. I'm doing this as a favor to Ross," he assured her. Tim's earnest eyes and soft voice mitigated his appearance and made him seem easily approachable.

"If it's not prying, may I ask why you're doing this for him?"

"I owe him a favor."

"It must have been a very great favor," she prompted.

"It was." That's what Ross had said. Shelley didn't want to give the subject up that easily, but Tim smiled and shook his head. "I promised I would never tell anyone what he did for me. I can only tell you that he's the truest friend a man can have, and that I would have achieved none of my accomplishments if it weren't for Ross and his generosity of spirit."

Shelley stared at him. "That's certainly a novel point of view," she said at last.

"Ah, you've heard that he's a cad, a bounder, a rogue."

"Something like that," Shelley admitted, amused at Tim's lexicon.

"You will only hear this kind of castigation from those who do not know him well, or those who are envious of him — for he is a man who appears to have everything."

"And doesn't he?" she asked curiously:

"But surely you should know, as the woman he is doing this for," said Tim in surprise.

"I . . . don't know him well, Tim, and frankly I'm convinced he has an ulterior motive for helping me like this."

Tim smiled. "He said you would say that."

"What else did he say?" she pounced.

"Nothing."

Shelley frowned.

"But surely a perceptive woman like you has seen the man of great needs and great gifts that lives beneath Ross's exterior!"

"Well, I . . . uh . . ." She stumbled over her words in confusion for a few more moments before deciding to give it up. She shrugged eloquently.

"Then you have barely scratched the surface, Michelle Baird. Which is a shame, because surely you deserve more. And so does he."

Intrigued, and rather eager to get some concrete information instead of cryptic comments, Shelley inquired, "Have you eaten yet, Tim? The least I can do is take you to lunch."

"I am meeting Ross shortly. He said to be sure to ask you to join us for lunch." Tim smiled. "He said you would refuse."

Shelley nearly said yes. She wanted to know what Ross was like with an old school friend. She wondered whether he would openly exhibit the qualities that Tim so clearly admired in him. But common sense prevailed. Particularly now that Ross was trying to buy her away from Babel, she just couldn't afford to be seen lunching with him again. She declined Tim's invitation with regret.

As Shelley bade Tim goodbye and showed him out the front door, both Francesca and Wayne stared with open curiosity.

"How did you find him so fast?" Wayne asked.

"Tanner," Shelley said shortly.

"Ross Tanner?" Wayne asked in total astonishment.

"Yes."

"That was a very beautiful man," Francesca said, referring to Tim.

"Yes," Shelley agreed.

"There have been some very remarkable men coming here lately," Francesca said with satisfaction.

"Yeah," said Wayne unenthusiastically. "Oh, for the good old days when women used to come here."

Shelley laughed and walked into her office. Wayne followed hot on her heels with Francesca right behind him.

Wayne wanted to know why Ross had done them such a favor. He examined all the possibilities. Was this a ploy to get Shelley interested in working for him? Was he trying to get them to lower their guard for some nefarious purpose? Was Tim indeed a competent interpreter of Pashto?

"Stay tuned for the answer to these and other questions," Shelley murmured, "same bat-time, same bat-channel."

"You're not contributing," Wayne complained.

"Maybe he just cares about Shelley," Francesca chirped maternally.

"Don't be ridiculous," Wayne snapped.

"I beg your pardon," said Shelley indignantly.

"He's a *businessman*, Shelley. A shrewd, cunning, relentless, insidious —"

"The man's a fiend!" cried Shelley.

Wayne looked at her in silence for a moment. "You think I'm overreacting, don't you?"

"Who, you?" She sat down at her desk. "I think that instead of speculating wildly, you should ask him personally."

"When do I ever see him?"

"This Thursday. He's holding an open house at Elite. I say we go find out what he's up to."

Ten minutes later Wayne left her office, rubbing his hands together and planning how he would cleverly, subtly trick Ross into revealing all his secret plans and schemes. Shelley shook her head in amusement. Wayne hoped to one day head Babel's central accounting office in New York. He still had a lot of maturing to do before he got there, she reflected.

*T*hursday arrived in the midst of a busy week at Babel. Tim had successfully completed his job for Shelley and headed back to California. The interpreters' coordinator in Washington thanked Shelley profusely for her help in the affair. She also confided to Shelley that she was about to hand in her resignation and move to Vermont; her analyst said the stress of her job was bad for her. Shelley also met again with Keene International, who still vacillated about their choice of language center.

"It's getting warmer, don't you think it's getting warmer?" said Wayne as he and Shelley walked to Elite that Thursday afternoon.

"Yes," she agreed. "Another week or two and I won't need a jacket."

Wayne opened the door to the Elite offices for her. She had to admire the new decor. The walls, floors, ceilings, and furniture were all done in complementing pastels, while several prints and vases stood out in bold, vivid color. It was simple, but the overall effect was one of elegance and extreme affluence. Shelley sighed glumly. This would all look great in Babel's lobby.

So would Ross, she realized with a sweet rush of sensation as her eyes met his. He returned his attention to the people he was talking to, but the mutual awareness which had plagued them since their first meeting was already flowing strongly between them.

She tried to tell herself that she wasn't disappointed that he hadn't called her, hadn't tried to see her, hadn't tried to change her sensible decision to stay away from him. But she wasn't much good at lying. Now that he was here, just a few steps away, her eyes feasted hungrily on the sight of him.

His black hair gleamed with healthy highlights, his tall, muscular body cut an impressive figure in his dark suit, his eyes sparkled with flirtatious amusement, and he exuded an aura of lazy, confident male magnetism.

Wow, she thought.

"Wow," said Wayne. "Look how many people are here."

There were indeed quite a lot of people. A significant number of them were Shelley's clients or potential clients. Common sense started intruding again. It would be unpardonably gauche and discourteous to do combat with Elite at their own party. However, she had to keep her clients from getting ensnared in Ross's silken web. This called for subtlety. She was sorry she had brought Wayne along.

"Shelley, I'm so glad you could make it." Ross came over and clasped her hand warmly in his. He was definitely on his worst behavior today. His eyes danced with delight, and she could see mischief and mayhem in their depths.

"Just trying to be polite to the underdog," she said sweetly. "You're making such an admirable effort here after sliding downhill for so long."

He grinned, enjoying her sally. "We appreciate your moral support," he said gravely.

"Wow, is that real champagne?" Wayne asked, looking at the refreshment table.

"Is there any other kind?" Ross asked dryly.

"Imported, too," Shelley murmured, eyeing the bottle being opened. The cork flew out with a discreet pop. "You must have quite a budget."

"I do. And, of course, I can arrange for the new director to have access to a healthy entertainment budget," he added meaningfully.

"Who's the new director?" Wayne asked eagerly.

Ross eyed Shelley with merciless delight. "I was frankly hoping —"

"Since Chuck has only just resigned, I'm sure it will take time for you to consider the prospects. Perhaps a transfer in from another Elite school?" Shelley gave him what she hoped was a look of bland curiosity.

"I have the perfect prospect in mind. You know that," he reminded her with insufferable innocence.

Shelley did her best to look blank. She had decided that her life would be considerably less complicated if no one knew about Ross's offer. She could have killed him for bringing it up again, especially here and now. He was certainly relentless; Wayne was right about that.

"Are you pleased with the turnout today?" she asked, changing the subject.

"Yes. It's too bad you didn't come earlier. We had quite a crowd."

"More than this?" Wayne asked.

"Lots more," Ross assured him, and named visitors from a dozen big companies, some of whom currently did business with Babel. "We're closing the doors soon," he added, looking at his watch.

"We meant to come earlier, but it was just such a busy day," Shelley said carefully.

"Being so understaffed can't make your job any easier," Ross said persistently.

"We can handle —" She stopped abruptly and looked across the crowded room, recognizing a familiar voice. Several teachers from her school, including Ute, the German teacher, were laughing and chatting with some Elite teachers. It was bad enough that her clients were here, but now so was her staff! And Ross had a well-deserved reputation for hiring away good staff from his competition, she thought ironically.

"Will you excuse me, please?" she said stiffly, and walked away.

Ross kept his eyes on Shelley as she made her way toward the teachers from her school. He had wondered how quickly she would notice them in the crowded lobby. Faster than most people would, he had guessed, and he was right.

Shelley's accountant, Wayne, the rather likeable epitome of a callow youth, distracted him briefly. Ross listened to the blond man soberly, hiding his amusement. With what Wayne no doubt believed was skillful subtlety and preternatural cunning, he started pumping Ross about his immediate plans for Elite.

Ross deftly avoided a number of the questions and responded to the rest with blatantly false information. He was good at verbal sparring — it was one of his best skills — so he was still able to devote most of his concentration to Shelley.

He was disproportionately pleased she had come and hoped she had missed seeing him as much as he had missed her. He wondered whether she was glad he had stayed away from her lately. He hadn't done it to be noble or to honor her wishes, and he was pretty sure she knew that. He doubted that she knew, however, that he'd stayed away because she'd given him the shock of his life.

"Are you considering any new teaching methods?" Wayne asked.

"Hmm, yes," Ross said absently. "The latest thing out of Paris is language instruction through hypnosis."

Wayne's eyes bulged.

Ross remembered those sweet moments with Shelley, those hot kisses stolen in the shadows of a busy street — something he hadn't done since he was a kid. What had she done to him? Suddenly there was a new depth between them, one he had never encountered anywhere or with anyone. Suddenly she had lain open every secret shadowy crevice of her soul and was demanding the same of him. Suddenly, in the middle of what should have been a casual embrace in broad daylight, she had scared the hell out of him.

She was so warm and giving. She didn't even know better than to give it all to a man like him. What exactly was she seeking in him? What if she didn't find it? He'd known from the first that she was different, that he couldn't keep her at arms' length if he wanted her, that there would be nothing casual about their relationship or easy about their parting.

He genuinely liked every woman he'd ever been involved with. But now he knew beyond the shadow of a doubt that a woman such as Shelley would require more than a little liking. What if he couldn't give more than that? What if he let her down? What if he hurt her?

"Language training with hypnosis must be very expensive," Wayne ventured.

"Oh, once we cover the cost of the psychic it's not too bad. All the equipment is being donated by a research institute."

Come on, Tanner, who are you kidding? he thought with self-disgust. What he was really afraid of was that *she* would hurt *him*. What if he let her get close and she didn't like what she saw? He'd always been in control of every relationship, and he knew instinctively that Shelley would make him toss control out the window in favor of honesty. What if he tried his best to give and take in an honest relationship, and she was disappointed in him? He winced inwardly at the thought. What if she was disgusted or disillusioned with the man beneath the guise? What if she wound up hating him?

Come on, get a grip, be a man if it kills you, he chided himself silently. Surely he had faced more intimidating prospects in his life than this small, earthy woman with her tumbling copper hair. But, looking across the room at her, none came to mind.

"Psychic?" Wayne questioned weakly. "Do you need a psychic for hypnosis?"

"For channeling. You know, in case the student spoke the target language in a past life. It makes things so much easier."

Wayne's jaw dropped. After a moment he narrowed his eyes and studied Ross with dawning suspicion. Ross smiled slightly. Shelley was right. He really was incorrigible.

Losing interest in the conversation, he glanced back at Shelley. Her spine had stiffened and she looked bemused. So Ute had broken the news, he thought. This might be a good chance to press his advantage with Shelley. However much he might want her — or want to run from her — personally, his attempt to hire her was still a good business decision. She really was the best. She would be a smashing success at Elite. He was sure that within a year she'd be promoted to a bigger school, perhaps to one of the ones he visited regularly for briefings and business meetings. . . .

He walked toward her, wondering whether this would be his chance to clinch the deal. As he approached, Shelley looked up at him. Her expression changed from one of patient understanding to one of barely controlled fury. One look at those big gray eyes burning with anger and hurt told him he'd miscalculated badly this time. He cursed her impractical sense of loyalty, even as he acknowledged that it was part of what made her so special.

"I am sorry, Shelley," Ute was saying. "You know it is not personal."

"Of course, Ute. I understand," Shelley said in such an even tone that Ross wondered whether anyone else realized how upset she was.

"But Ross has offered me the pay that Babel should be giving me after all the years I have worked for them."

"I know. You have to choose the employer you feel is fairest," Shelley answered calmly.

"You know I like working for you, Shelley. If only they weren't so inflexible at headquarters . . ."

Shelley looked at Ross with ill-concealed hostility. "Congratulations, Ross. You've just hired an excellent German teacher."

"If Babel won't pay its employees what they deserve, it can't reasonably expect to keep them," Ross said with quiet force. His oblique reference to her own position only seemed to make her angrier.

"Have you also hired a Japanese teacher today?" she asked steadily, looking at the pretty, young Japanese woman who worked for her.

Hiroko shrugged, looking distressed. "I don't know, Shelley. I don't want to quit you, but he's offering better pay. I've got to pay my tuition, my car, my rent . . . I just don't know."

"Me, I will stay with Shelley," said Pablo Gutierrez. "You saved my neck, no?" he added with a grin.

Shelley smiled gratefully at him. Her other teachers shifted uncomfortably. "Look, gang, I didn't come here to make a scene. I wish I could convince you to stay at Babel. I'll keep trying to talk New York into raising your pay. But . . . you have your own lives and pocketbooks to consider, and I certainly can't blame you for being enticed by Elite's promises of higher pay. Just come and talk to me first, okay? If only to say goodbye."

Shelley turned away from the group. She felt a pressing need to get out of the room, away from all of them, away from Ross.

"Can we talk about this?" he said, following her.

"No!" she said sharply. "Just leave me alone."

She saw Wayne embroiled in conversation with some woman and decided to leave without interrupting him. She had to get out of here. She needed time to regroup. It was the end of a long day, and she was too overworked to cope rationally with this right now.

She went directly to the coat closet and rifled through it, looking for the beige jacket she'd hung up upon arriving. As she ripped it off the hanger, strong hands took it away from her. She looked up into Ross's serious gaze.

"Will you come into my office and talk privately with me?"

"So you can justify this with your verbal acrobatics?"

"You're being —"

"Don't you dare tell me I'm being unreasonable," she snapped.

"Your teachers are smart enough —"

"*I* am not an underpaid part-time employee just passing through, so don't equate me with them. I'm the director. I'm the captain of the ship that you're sinking, and I do *not* want to talk again about why I should desert it to come to work for the guy who's masterminding this *blitzkrieg*!" She tried to yank her coat away from him.

He held it open for her, a frown creasing his brow as she thrust her arms inside the sleeves and pulled away from him. "What has Babel ever done to make you so damn loyal?" he demanded.

"How can you talk about it that way? As if there's something wrong with my sticking with it?" she retorted.

"To the bitter and inevitable end," he snapped:

"Spoken like a man who has never seen *anything* through to the end," Shelley said as a parting shot, and stormed out the door.

As the door swung shut behind her, something uncontrollable escaped inside of Ross. He didn't know whether it was caused by the sight of her walking out of his office — and very probably out of his life — for good, or a deeply personal reaction to the insult she'd just flung in his face. Or even a simple desire to comfort her for what he inevitably had to do to her business.

All he knew was he couldn't let her get away that easily. Not after all the sleep he'd lost over her. Not after all the questions she'd raised in his mind. Not after all the desire she'd stirred in his body. He brusquely told his astonished secretary to lock up when she left and walked out of his own party.

Shelley hadn't even reached the street corner yet when she realized she wasn't alone. She glanced behind her in time to see Ross catch up with her just as she stopped to wait for the light. She glared at him in exasperation.

"You can't take a hint, can you? You can't even take a rude dismissal! Is the word 'no' anywhere in your vocabulary? In any language?" she raged, throwing her arms up.

"In twenty-seven languages, actually."

"Don't start with me!"

"It's too late, we've already started. This is something I'm going to see through to the end," he said grimly.

She looked at him and suddenly felt embarrassed. "I'm sorry I said that," she said in a much softer voice. "It was an inexcusably personal criticism based on . . . on a written report put together by strangers."

Her unprofessional rage about his trying to hire her, her sudden regret for hurting him and the wary glow in her gray eyes reached out to Ross and gave him a sudden surge of cocky confidence. He wasn't the only one who was scared of what was happening between them. He suddenly believed everything would be all right.

"Have dinner with me," he urged.

"Stay away from me," Shelley answered, and stepped off the curb.

"Shelley!" He grabbed her arm and pulled her backward before she was flattened by the rush-hour traffic. "Are the words 'don't walk' anywhere in your vocabulary?" he chided.

"Don't you have a party to host?"

"It's almost over. Besides, I've accomplished everything I wanted to get done today. Except for getting through to you."

"Don't count on it," she said as the light changed. She stepped off the curb and walked as fast as she could.

"What are we doing this evening?" he asked lightly, easily keeping pace with her.

"*We* are not doing anything. *I* am going to pamper myself to make up for all the stress I've been under since you came to town."

"Pamper? How?" He eyed her figure appreciatively. "I could give you a rubdown."

"Go away," she said, enunciating the words slowly and clearly. "*Va t'en.* Split. *Vai via. Am-scray.* Be gone with you."

"*No. Nein. Non. Lo.* Negative. Forget it. No way, baby."

She stared at him stonily. "I have reached a new depth of sympathy for your parents," she said at last.

He gave her his most smoldering look. "Has anyone ever told you you're beautiful when you're angry?"

"Urrgh," Shelley said and turned to enter the clothing boutique they were standing in front of. Unperturbed, Ross followed her inside.

He pursued her to a rack of dreary tan skirts. He frowned. He couldn't, in good conscience, let her waste her hard-earned money on something that ugly.

"Not that you've asked, or even given me the benefit of the doubt," he said conversationally as Shelley looked through a row of boring white pullovers, "but I didn't purposely steal Ute away from you. She came to see me earlier this week to apply for a job. Of course, we talked about her circumstances. She likes you and is unhappy about leaving, but she's right, Shelley. Babel should pay her more."

"Until you came, Chuck's teachers made *less* than my teachers. Don't try to pretend to me that Elite has a higher moral sense than my bosses. You're just raising everyone's pay here because it's expedient." She picked up a brown dress that was much too long for a woman of her petite size.

"That's true," he admitted, "but you can hardly blame the teachers for jumping on the bandwagon. They've got to eat. And I didn't invite the other teachers to the open house today. Ute did."

"But you went ahead and told them how much you'd pay them."

"Of course I did. That's what they came to find out. Be reasonable, Shelley."

"Don't say that to me again. Anyhow the working day is over. I don't have to be reasonable or polite or understanding if I don't feel like it. And I definitely don't."

"I'll watch my step."

"Just see that you do." Shelley held up a sensible tweed skirt that would do nothing for her lovely coloring or the smoothly feminine swell of her hips. Ross couldn't stand it anymore.

"You're not going to try that on, are you?" he demanded.

"Well . . . yes," she said, surprised by his exasperated tone.

"Absolutely not," Ross said, taking the skirt away from her.

"What are you doing?" She looked at him in confusion.

"Shelley, Shelley . . ." He shook his head, a pained expression on his face.

"What?" Her eyes narrowed. She wondered whether he was up to something again.

"Didn't anyone ever explain these things to you?"

"What things?"

"Look," he said, dragging her in front of a mirror. "Look and tell me what you see."

"Ross, how much champagne did you have?"

He held her still and looked at her reflection with her. "Pale skin. Gray eyes. Copper hair, lots of it. Short stature."

"Petite," she amended.

"Of course, forgive me. Petite. Beautifully rounded."

"Is that a wisecrack?"

"With all this good raw material, why smother it in drab clothes that do nothing for you?"

"You have some nerve —"

"Shelley, it would be immoral of me to let you buy any of the things you've been looking at since we walked in here."

"You have no business —" She looked at him, suddenly remembering that his mother was French. He'd probably been around when she was teaching his two sisters these things. French women were always the best dressers. She'd be a fool to let this opportunity slip by. As casually as she could, she said, "What would you suggest?"

He grinned. Shelley scowled. He'd probably be insufferable about this. "I thought you'd never ask," he teased.

"Well?" she challenged.

"Let's see . . ." He took her hand and looked around the store. He led her to several more racks of clothing, obviously seeing nothing that satisfied him. Shelley glanced longingly at a couple of sturdy, simple items that had been marked down. "Absolutely not," Ross said inflexibly.

Finally he discovered something: a blue-gray cashmere dress with a narrow belt and wide neckline.

"I can't wear this, Ross," she protested. "It has no shape."

"Can it possibly have escaped your notice all these years that you have plenty of shape? You look like my adolescent fantasies."

"I don't think —"

"And there's no point in hiding the best curves I've ever seen under tweed skirts and starched blouses."

She finally agreed to try the dress on, only because she realized that a number of saleswomen and customers were listening with fascination to his comments about her body. He insisted she come out of the dressing room to show him how the dress looked, and he gloated when Shelley admitted that it was the best she'd looked in years. The blue-gray color highlighted her eyes better than make-up and brought out the darker red shades in her hair. The soft cashmere clung to every line and curve, making her look somehow slimmer and shapelier at the same time, and the style made her look just a fraction taller.

She studied the neckline with a thoughtful frown. Although it emphasized her delicate collarbones, there was certainly nothing immodest or suggestive about it. She could easily wear this dress to work.

"If the shop owner had seen that dress on you first, she'd be charging twice the price," Ross assured her. His eyes gleamed with an admiration that made Shelley flush.

"Even at this price it's a bit steep," she said softly. She took one more look in the mirror. "But I have to have it." She glanced at him hesitantly. "Have you . . . uh . . . seen anything else I might want to try on?"

He smiled knowingly and handed her three more items he'd noticed while waiting for her to change. She tried each one on and dutifully came out of the dressing room each time to get his opinion. He was aware that everyone in the shop had grown interested in their quest by now, but it didn't bother him. He was enjoying himself and he thought it was about time Shelley started realizing how beautiful she really was.

"Why did you pick this one? I can't wear something like this," Shelley insisted as she stepped out of the dressing room wearing the last of the clothes he'd selected for her.

Ross caught his breath. Even he hadn't realized what she would do for the simple little black silk dress. She had such a strong effect on him.

"You look beautiful." He heard the husky rasp of his own voice. Shelley looked at him curiously. What was there about this woman that always melted his practiced *savoir-faire*? Her plump breasts pushed upward against the low-cut dress, her smooth, firm flesh calling forth fantasies he couldn't seem to control. He saw himself slipping the spaghetti straps off her gleaming white shoulders, saw himself pulling the short skirt up over her hips to touch and explore and —

"Are you listening to me?" she prodded.

"Sorry, what?" he asked, uncomfortably aware of the sudden snugness of his trousers. The tailor hadn't taken Shelley Baird into account when he'd made them, Ross thought ruefully. *Slow down, you can't throw her to the floor and ravish her here.* That would be a definite *faux pas.*

"I said it's lovely, Ross, but I haven't got any use for a dress like this."

"We'll find a use for it," he assured her, his fantasies bursting back to life despite his best efforts to quell them. *Shelley, what have I been afraid of? It's going to be so damn good between us.*

"Take it, honey," said one of the other customers suddenly. "Your man knows what he's talking about. I only wish I could look half as good as you in that dress."

"Oh. Thank you," Shelley said weakly. Her man? To avoid looking at Ross, she looked in the mirror again. That clinched it. So what if she couldn't afford it? So what if she'd probably never have a chance to wear it? It was the most beautiful thing she'd ever worn, and she was here to pamper herself. Suddenly full of firm and decadent resolve, she said, "Yes, I'll take it."

"Thank you," said Ross.

She glanced up at him. Her blood raced through her veins and she felt her face flush. She suddenly knew why he'd chosen this dress, knew what plans he had for her in it. It was written all over his face, overwhelming his usually controlled features. His look of raw desire burned through her, thrilling her, frightening her. She felt a sudden contraction deep inside her most secret places. A moist throbbing started within her, a persistent ache that only he could reach. And he could reach it only by —

She drew a quick, sharp breath. She saw in his eyes that he'd read her thoughts. He knew. He was thinking the same thing.

They were through playing games, he realized. She was ready. And he couldn't wait for her any longer.

Their gazes held for a moment longer, and Ross saw the sudden acceptance, the calm decision in hers. They had both already passed their last chance to make a clean escape; they were past even wanting to.

"I'll hand this dress and the others out to you," Shelley said softly. "Take them up to the counter and tell the girl to get them ready." Ross nodded. "Oh, and tell her . . . tell her I'll pay by credit card." She didn't add that she'd be paying off that bill for the rest of her natural life.

Shelley took her time putting on her own clothes in the dressing room. It was a he-knew-she-knew-he-knew situation. There was no point in pretending they didn't both know what was going to happen between them, and soon. They'd pretended long enough. But she needed a little time to compose herself. Finally realizing she wasn't going to get any more composed, she went back out into the dress shop.

Ross was holding a shiny bag full of her beautiful new clothes.

"I have to pay for them," she said, still speaking softly, wondering what had happened to her usual tone of voice.

"I've already paid," he said just as quietly.

Their eyes met. She could say she couldn't accept such a gift from him. She could say she was an independent woman who could pay for her own wardrobe. She could even rage that he had no right to be so presumptuous.

She said, "Thank you."

They'd already silently made and agreed upon their decision. It didn't matter that nothing concrete had yet been said or done. Whatever the future held in store for them, they both knew that he had just become the one man in her life who had the right to buy her costly gifts.

He held the door open for her and then followed her out into the darkening street. They were both being awfully quiet for two talkative people. Shelley didn't feel like talking about trivial things and couldn't yet find the words to discuss what mattered. Silence was best for a few minutes, and Ross seemed to sense this, too. She went along willingly with him, not bothering to ask where they were going. Several blocks later they reached his red Porsche, which was parked in one of the city's many small lots.

He put her package behind the driver's seat and then looked at her over the roof of the car. He must be slightly unnerved, she thought fondly; he'd forgotten to open her door for her.

"Where do you want to eat?" he asked.

"Mount Adams." There would be no chance of accidentally running into any of her staff or clients up there, as there would be downtown.

He nodded, and she realized he knew the reason behind her request. They'd have to talk about it. They'd have to talk about a lot of things. Later, she thought, later. For the moment they just needed to get adjusted to this. They were together now.

She slid into her seat. He turned on the engine. He looked over his shoulder, preparatory to putting the car into reverse.

"Wait," she said suddenly. She needed something. Some affirmation, some comfort. Her eyes met his.

"Shelley," he whispered. His voice held a tenderness she'd never heard before, and his eyes were openly vulnerable.

She leaned toward him, lowering her eyes, seeking his lips with her own. He returned her kiss with exquisite tenderness, with painful longing, with a special kind of friendship.

They leaned their foreheads together, each savoring the other's nearness.

"When the gods want to punish us, they answer our prayers," he murmured wryly.

Shelley voiced the same sentiment in her more down-to-earth way: "Are we in *it.*"

$MARK

Seven

"*E*verything I've ever heard or read about you tells me you can't be fired. *My* job isn't so sacred," Shelley said steadily.

Ross looked out at the spectacular nighttime view of the Ohio River Valley. They were seated in one of Shelley's favorite restaurants atop Mount Adams, not far from her apartment. They had ordered food and wine and were feeling more prepared to confront the issues between them.

"You don't want anyone to know about us, in other words."

"I think it could cost me my position, if I were known to be . . ." she trailed off.

"Sleeping with me?" he supplied, unwilling to let her even hint that their relationship might be anything less serious.

She nodded. "On the other hand it just seems so sleazy to keep it a big secret."

He shrugged. "Let's just agree to keep it a secret one day at a time. You can wake up any morning and change your mind. I, on the other hand, don't care who knows, as long as it doesn't hurt you."

She nodded again. "And I think we'd better agree not to talk about work."

"Do you think that's possible?"

"I think if we do, we'll just go round and round the way we've been doing since you got here. I think it's best if we just draw a clean line between our jobs and our relationship."

"And what happens if we have more confrontations in our professional capacities?"

"I think we should . . . leave it at the office and not bring it home with us." She saw the concern in his eyes and shrugged uncomfortably. "I don't know if I can, but I'll try."

They were silent again. They both knew that most of the pressure she would be under in the coming weeks would be because of him. They both knew that he could ruin her career at Babel. He was frustrated that she simply wouldn't consider a career with Elite as a reasonable alternative; she was frustrated that he couldn't understand why.

And under all that they both knew that Ross would only be in the same city with her as long as it took to establish supremacy for Elite here. But despite everything they couldn't stay away from each other any longer. . . .

Ross poured more wine. Shelley nibbled at the appetizer they'd ordered. She caught him staring at her. They both started smiling foolishly. She was so glad to be with him like this at last!

"Tell me honestly —"

"Honestly?" he repeated doubtfully.

"Why did you send for Tim to help me out?"

He tilted his head to one side and let his eyes caress her. She warmed to his perusal, finally enjoying rather than resisting the pleasure his admiring gaze gave her.

"For you, Shelley. Just to help you. No other reason. No 'ulterior motives.' I can't . . .be inadequate at my job for your sake, but this was something I could do for you without compromising my integrity."

She realized that she'd never heard him talk about his integrity before. She sensed such seriousness didn't come easily to the surface with him. She was sorry she had simply assumed at times that he didn't possess any integrity merely because he didn't parade it around. She let her eyes tell him so.

"What did you do for Tim? Oh, come on, Ross," she urged, seeing he meant to refuse to answer. "You can tell me."

He shrugged, taking another sip of wine. "I saved his neck once, that's all."

"How?"

He smiled. "There was an incident at college. I got expelled for it, actually —"

"Ah, yes. Your famous aphrodisiac."

"You know about that?" he said in surprise. "Well, yes, I guess that's something Babel could find out about pretty easily. It got a lot of publicity at the time."

"How was Tim involved?"

"Well, I had developed an obscure major in Middle Eastern philosophy, designed purely for the purpose of showing my family that nothing, but nothing, was going to make me fall in line with their plans for me."

Shelley smiled, remembering her own estimate of that.

"And in some obscure old text I read about this strange aphrodisiac. The author made some claims about it that a gentleman really can't repeat to a lady." Shelley rolled her eyes.

"Anyhow," he continued. "I showed the passage to Tim, just for a laugh. He was a biochemistry major at the time. He was convinced we could duplicate it and make a fortune selling it to fraternity boys. A few of the ingredients puzzled him, but he thought he could come up with reasonable substitutes."

"Oh, my goodness," Shelley said slowly.

"I just kind of tagged along. Not innocently, to be honest. I mean, I was always getting into trouble in those days. But I was frankly expecting a dull time watching Tim play with beakers and test tubes." He grinned at her. "I take it you know what happened after that?"

"All hell broke loose."

"Exactly. We both got caught red-handed. I felt so sorry for Tim. He'd never been in trouble before, whereas I was used to it. He was terrified. I think he was afraid that his family would make him return to Afghanistan if they heard about the incident. So I took all the blame. I told the Dean that Tim had just been innocently doing some make-up work for a class, and that I'd been the only one to make unauthorized use of university property."

"That was very nice of you."

"Not really. Like I said, I was used to trouble. Of course, I didn't realize I'd get expelled for it."

"Were you upset?" Shelley asked.

"Surprised, mostly. I'd intentionally done a lot of things I knew I wasn't supposed to, and now I'd finally gotten kicked out for something I hadn't intended to happen. But once I started thinking about it, I was glad. I knew my family couldn't fix it. I'd be on my own. Finally."

"Did Tim —"

"Oh, sure. When he realized I was going to be expelled, he wanted to share my shame. But that would have been a waste, and I made him promise to never tell anyone. It was the right decision, too. Here he is all these years later, a serious man with an impressive academic career. Whereas I probably never would have finished college."

"Was that when Tim switched his major to English lit?"

"Yes."

They both laughed. Shelley studied Ross consideringly. For all her intuition, she had understood so little about him. Tim had been right. Ross was a man of generous spirit, of great gifts. And of great needs? she wondered.

"Looking back now," he mused, "I can see it was the best thing that ever happened to me."

"Why?" she asked curiously.

"Well, my family kicked me out on my ear — we, uh, had some words about the incident and my general character, and I acted as badly as usual. Being left to my own devices at nineteen, as well as having all financial support withdrawn, turned out to be very good for me. It was about the only chance I had of acquiring any character."

"Do you really believe that?"

"Absolutely. I was spoiled, bored, careless, selfish, and thoughtless. I had a lot of very unattractive character traits, and you should know going into this, Shelley, that I haven't discarded all of them yet. I'd had everything a boy could ever want. I'd been given more second chances than you could count. I was bright enough to succeed at school but too bloody stubborn to bother most of the time. I was a rich boy, so there were plenty of girls —"

"Trust me when I say your money had nothing to do with *that,*" Shelley said dryly. "But how did you get to be such a . . . brat?"

"Just came naturally to me, I guess."

"Come on," she insisted.

"I shouldn't have been born with all that. I would have been better off if I'd always had to work my butt off — like you."

"It's character building," she admitted.

"And I wasn't cut out to be what my father wanted me to be."

"Which was?"

"His successor, in every way. You can pound a lot of good manners and expensive tastes and correct speech into a kid, but you can't turn him inside out and make him what he's not."

"No. Especially not someone like you."

"I'm just not proper."

"Who, you?" she said blandly.

"I wanted adventure. I like change. Till the day I die, I'll like stirring up trouble. My dad's work seemed incredibly dreary to me, the people he dealt with bored me to distraction, and our social position strangled me. I started going my own way when I was about four years old. Since I was the only son, he wouldn't give up on me. God forbid he should let one of his daughters take his place instead of me," Ross said, some of his old exasperation showing up in his expression.

"Your poor mother. Your house must have been a war zone."

He looked sheepish. "It was. She wanted peace between us, but it just couldn't happen. The harder he pushed, the more I rebelled. I even did things I didn't want to do, just to show him there was no way I'd do what *he* wanted me to do."

"So what happened when he kicked you out after you were expelled?" she asked.

"My sisters were upset, but my mom was devastated. I was too young and selfish to think about how they felt. I just disappeared. Free at last."

"Where did you go?" she prodded.

"Well, I thought about going to Provence. I'd always been very close to my French relatives, always happiest during the summers I spent with them. But that seemed like it would be cowardly. I'd done everything I could for nineteen years to make my family give up on me. I figured I might as well get on with my new life as an orphan."

He grinned at her and continued. "It gets pretty weird after that. I worked some odd jobs for a while. I have a distant uncle that no one ever talked to because he was a smuggler. So, of course, I hunted him up. He had a ship, a rustbucket really, that plied the Mediterranean and the west coast of Africa."

"Did you really smuggle?" Shelley asked in fascination.

"Mostly we hauled regular cargo. But sometimes we smuggled wine, whiskey, tobacco, pistachio nuts, exotic oils, artifacts. Once we even hauled a load of some dreadful liquor made out of bananas that went bad halfway through the trip. Lord, was I sick!"

"Did you like that life?"

"I was usually in too much pain to worry about liking it." He smiled reminiscently, recalling his initiation. "It was a tougher life than I'd ever known. I worked so hard that some nights I didn't have the strength to pull the blanket over myself before I fell asleep. At first my hands were raw with blisters for weeks. It took a while for me to develop all the muscle and calluses and stamina I needed for that life. Not to mention the nerve. More than once I was afraid I'd rot in a third world prison. And I looked like the spoiled, fresh-faced kid I was, so I got robbed and beat up a lot at first."

"How long did you stick with it?"

"Until I was good at it. I was determined to conquer or die. I got to be the toughest, shrewdest, most slippery guy my dear old uncle knew. By the end of my second year with him I decided I'd learned enough and that this wasn't the life for which I'd rebelled against my father for nineteen years. I quit."

"Gosh, Ross, this is better than going to the movies."

"You haven't touched your dinner," he pointed out. "It's been sitting in front of you for five minutes. Eat something."

She put some food into her mouth, scarcely tasting it. "Well? What did you do then?"

"Oh, a lot of things. I started showing tourists around different countries in the Mediterranean. Just offered my services to people. I knew where they could find what they wanted, whether they were interested in fine food, good beaches, nightlife, rare artifacts. I worked for about five months as an interpreter and sort of general assistant for a British movie company in Morocco. Then I started working in a casino in Marrakech. I wound up running it after the manager disappeared mysteriously. People tended to do that a lot there, it seemed. I turned that shabby little casino into a great success in about a year. We even started attracting lots of Europeans who were 'slumming.'"

"And you gave it up when you decided that that wasn't why you'd left your family, either."

"It was all getting pretty sordid. I decided it was time to be near my relatives in Provence, make peace with my mom and dad. I got work after a while —"

"Managing a nightclub."

"A pretty tawdry one, to be honest."

"Did you sort out your family problems?" '

"With everyone but my dad. We just called a cease-fire. We're civil to each other, even talk now and then. We just weren't cut out to be close, though."

"And after Nice?"

"I went to Paris. I was tired of living on the seamy side of life. It had been good for me. It had even been fun. But I wanted to live in nice places, meet normal people again, tell them what I did for a living. I still had expensive tastes and I decided there was nothing wrong with that. Unfortunately, though, I still couldn't stand to be under authority of any kind. I lost two jobs in two months."

"I can believe that," she admitted. It was impossible to picture Ross taking orders from anyone. She smiled fondly, adoring him, so pleased to have all those gaps in his past filled in, so sorry she hadn't seen his courage and self-honesty before. She reached across the table to lightly stroke his cheek. His eyes softened, and she could see the gesture pleased him. He pressed a kiss into her palm. "Then what?"

"Then Henri hired me," he said simply.

"Why? I mean, you couldn't have seemed very promising."

"Well, he didn't exactly *hire* me," Ross admitted.

"Oh?"

"No. I sort of won the job in a poker game."

"Really? Ross, this is great!"

"I knew I had a touch for figuring out why a place was losing money and how to turn it around. I'd done it in Marrakech and again in Nice, but I wanted a respectable job this time, as well as my independence. I found myself in a poker game with Henri Montpazier and saw my chance. When the stakes got high enough, I made an interesting offer. If I lost, I'd work for him for free for one year. If I won, he'd pay me a good salary and give me one year to prove I could turn around the most disastrous school in his business empire. I won," he added smugly.

Shelley stared at him incredulously. "*That* was the beginning of your career with Elite? That's incredible! No wonder you're outside the chain of command," she mused.

"Shelley? This isn't fodder for your business. This is between us, remember?" he reminded her with mock-severity.

"Yes, yes, yes." She attacked her dinner enthusiastically. His story had answered so many of her questions about him. For the moment there was just one more. "Who else have you told this to? I mean . . . all of this?"

"I know what you mean." His eyes met hers. "You're the only person who knows *all* of it, Shelley. There's an awful lot that I'm not proud of and don't talk much about. I told you, I had to learn things the hard way. But . . . I'll tell you the truth about anything you want to know."

Her eyes were equally serious as she said, "Thank you. I'm glad."

His mood changed, and his eyes sparkled as he asked, "But tell me, how did a nice girl like you get involved in a racket like this?"

"It's a very dull story compared to yours. I was a tour guide for a number of years in Europe. I started out by working for peanuts during the summers while I was in college. After college I got a real job. I loved to travel. I liked working with people and I even liked it when things went wrong, because it was a challenge. I opted for fun jobs rather than ones that paid well, so I was always broke. I had a cot in a corner of a crowded flat in Paris, but I was almost never there. I did the circuits almost nonstop for five years: Great Britain, France, Belgium, Luxembourg, Spain, Italy."

"I take it the gypsy life palled after awhile?"

"Oh, yes. I started having trouble remembering which city I was in or what language I was supposed to use. I grew to hate suitcases, hotels, backpacks, campsites, buses, campers, roads, restaurants — anything that was even remotely associated with travel. I took a leave of absence and went back to Chicago to spend some time with my family and think over my future. I was so glad to have some stability back in my life that I decided I'd had enough. It was a good run, but it was over."

"That was when you got a job with Babel?"

"Yes. I applied to Elite and a number of other places in Chicago, as well," she said significantly. "But Babel hired me first. I started out teaching and doing a bit of office work. Everyone kept quitting, and within a year I was the assistant director. When the director of the Cincinnati school was fired, Jerome, my boss in Chicago, recommended they promote me and give me the job. He really pushed hard, because headquarters thought I was too young and too inexperienced. But they gave me the post in the end. And I've done a good job."

"A very good job. I might not even be here if you weren't doing such a good job."

She sighed. "Ironic, isn't it?"

Unlike their silence earlier in the evening, they seemed unable to stop talking now. They told stories about the past, shared memories of their favorite places, laughed about some mistakes they'd made and honestly admitted their regret about others. Shelley marveled at all he'd been through, at all the complex facets of Ross Tanner. No wonder she'd been irresistibly drawn to him the first time she'd laid eyes on him. He was even more extraordinary than she had guessed.

He was still a flirt, still a smooth talker, and nearly every gesture bore the mark of his privileged upbringing. But there was so much more to him than the casual elegance and easy charm she'd first noticed. Whatever happened between them professionally she was glad fate had thrown this remarkable man in her path.

The restaurant was quiet and nearly empty when Ross finally noticed their waitress casting meaningful looks in their direction. "I think we've overstayed our welcome," he said to Shelley.

"What time is it?" She looked at her watch. "I can't believe it! It's past midnight!"

Ross looked around. "No wonder everyone else is gone."

"I've got to get home, Ross. I have so much to do in the morning. I have to —" She stopped abruptly. It was there between them. She refused to let it spoil even a moment of their time together. She smiled instead. "We'd better pay up and go."

Ross left a very generous tip on the table to compensate for staying all evening. He helped Shelley on with her light jacket, and they walked out to his car. "I think I remember how to get there," he said when she started to direct him to her apartment.

"Don't bother to hunt for a parking place," Shelley said as they neared her building. "Just drop me off at the front door."

He stopped the car and looked into her eyes. She met his gaze squarely, neither embarrassed nor uncomfortable with the question she saw there. "Not tonight?" he asked softly.

"Soon," she promised.

"I . . . need it to be soon." His voice was husky with emotion.

"So do I," she admitted. "But . . .well, if you think about it, this was our first real date."

He had to smile. "You have such a way of putting things into perspective. But I'll lay awake all night wanting you and thinking about how good it's going to be."

She swallowed, heat rushing through her. "Do you . . ."

"What?"

"Sleep naked?" she asked at last, dying to know.

His eyes gleamed. "Yes. Do you?"

"No. I always thought if there were a fire or I suddenly developed appendicitis —"

He chuckled. "Ever practical. Let's make a deal for tonight."

"What?"

"Let's both sleep naked. It'll at least give us something to think about, since you're going to be such a killjoy tonight."

"Don't be annoyed, Ross."

"I'm not," he assured her. "I'm disappointed. But, believe it or not, I understand. On the other hand, some heavy petting . . ."

"In this car?" she asked incredulously.

"No, I guess you're right," he sighed. "It's pretty — cramped in here for that sort of thing. And somebody could get hurt by that stick shift."

"Now don't be vulgar," she chided.

He grinned mischievously. "I know, I'm incorrigible. It's one of those faults I can't seem to shake."

"I'm getting used to it," she said fatalistically.

"I'll call you tomorrow. We'll make plans for tomorrow night."

"Okay." She leaned over to kiss him.

His mouth slid over hers in moist, lazy circles, nibbling and tasting and teasing.

"Oh, you're so good at this," she sighed.

"I'm just warming up," he promised her. His tongue slipped delicately into her mouth and greeted hers with soft, satiny caresses. His hand slid down to her breast and massaged it, touching her possessively, confidently establishing his right to do so.

She felt her nipples hardening, felt the persistent throb deep inside her grow to an ache only he could assuage. Erotic images of him in her bedroom tumbled through her mind. She was on the verge of telling him to come upstairs with her when he pulled away abruptly.

He didn't try to disguise his labored breathing or the depth of his desire. He simply whispered, "Soon," and reached across her to open her door.

"Good morning," Shelley said brightly as she encountered Wayne and Francesca near the coffee maker at Babel the next morning.

They both murmured good morning and said nothing more. Nobody talked about the open house at Elite. Nobody complimented Shelley on her new dress. Nobody remarked on how happy she looked. In fact they both avoided looking at her.

Always one for the direct approach, Shelley said, "What's wrong?"

Francesca smiled tremulously then glanced nervously at Wayne.

"Where were you last night?" Wayne asked heavily.

Shelley froze. "Why?"

Francesca and Wayne glanced at each other again. "When I realized you'd left Elite without me I asked around. The secretary said you'd left with Tanner."

"I didn't leave with —"

"No, actually she said you both tried to make it appear as if you were leaving separately. She said that Charles said that the two of you have gone out together before."

"We have, but it was a business lunch," she began.

"So how come you never told me about it?" he challenged.

"Because . . . I didn't accomplish anything." She realized how phony that sounded. "Oh, the hell with it. It was because he offered me Chuck's job with double the pay and benefits I get now, and I didn't want you to worry about it."

"Are you taking it?" Francesca asked, wide-eyed.

"No, of course not."

"Then what were you doing with him last night?" Wayne asked angrily.

"I — We — Oh, I can't explain it."

"I thought nothing of it, at first. I was dying to know what you two talked about, in fact, figuring it had to be business. So I called your house. Again and again. Until well after midnight, Shelley. I even called his hotel, because I was a little worried, but he hadn't returned to his suite."

"We were having dinner."

"Six hours is an awfully long business dinner." The words hung heavily in the air. Francesca's eyes darted nervously from Wayne to Shelley and back again. Finally Wayne said, "It wasn't a business dinner, was it?"

"No, it wasn't," Shelley said quietly.

"You're seeing him?"

"Yes." So much for keeping it a big secret.

She could see that despite understandable doubts, Francesca was happy for her. Wayne, on the other hand, was not.

"Are you crazy?" he demanded.

"Maybe," she said wearily, all her joy in Ross turning sour.

"Shelley, even if he's being sincere, which I doubt —"

"He is!" she insisted hotly.

"*If* he is, do you honestly think you can do this? How do we know you won't cave in and let him ruin us completely here because you're so infatuated with him?"

"I won't. Our relationship has nothing to do with business!"

"How can it not, Shelley? Who do you think you're kidding?"

"After everything I've accomplished here, I would think you'd have more faith in my professionalism than that."

"And do you think headquarters will, after all they've said about him? After everything he's done to our business in other cities? Do you think they'll believe for a moment that you're still being loyal to them?"

"Stop it!" Shelley said, hating him for voicing all the fears she had firmly pushed aside last night.

"How do you think Jerome will feel, since he's the one who got you this job in the first place? He'll take a lot of flak for this."

She tried to regain control of herself. "Are headquarters going to hear about this?" She met Wayne's gaze levelly. "Is Jerome?"

"Are you going to ask me not to tell him?"

"No. *Are* you going to tell him?"

Wayne turned away from her and crumpled his paper coffee cup. He shoved his hands in his pockets, then pulled them back out. "Shelley, don't do this to me. Don't ask me to cover for you."

"Okay, I won't."

"I have a career to think about, too."

"I know."

"You can't keep something like this a secret for long."

Not even for twenty-four hours, she thought sadly.

"When Jerome finds out, he'll also find out that I knew it and did nothing," Wayne continued.

There was a long, heavy silence. Shelley felt an unbearable tension building inside of her, threatening to snap and shatter her into a thousand pieces. She felt absurdly guilty, as if she were indeed failing in her commitments, as if her feelings for Ross were sordid and sleazy and wrong. She and Wayne had never been close friends, but they had always been a solid working team. There had never been dissent or distrust inside the walls of her school before. She wanted to cry.

"Are you going to stop seeing him?" Wayne asked.

Shelley was silent. She wanted to say yes, to promise she would never see Ross again.

"For God's sake, Shelley, can't you control this?" he exclaimed.

She shrugged. She had tried so hard to control it.

"Why don't you just take his job offer? Then you could do whatever you wanted with him, and no one would care"

"Wayne!" Francesca interjected. "Don't say any more right now. You are both too upset."

Shelley raised hurt, embarrassed eyes to Wayne's face. She saw the mistrust in his expression. She saw his doubt in her integrity, her loyalty, her capability.

"You'd better call Chicago now," she whispered.

"Damn you," he snarled, and stormed out of the room. She heard him slam the door of his office a moment later.

"He is overreacting," Francesca said comfortingly.

"Is he?" Shelley asked weakly. "Do you think Jerome will think so? Do you think headquarters will think so?"

"I think," Francesca said calmly, "that you had no choice in this matter. I think from the first time I saw Ross with you, I knew this was inevitable between you. *Che sarà, sarà.*"

Shelley smiled faintly. "Thank you."

The rest of the day went downhill from there. Hiroko and Pablo arrived to teach lessons. Their wary, curious eyes told Shelley that they, too, knew she had left Elite with Ross. Since the tension at Babel was thick enough to swim in, and since Ross's secretary was obviously a nasty gossip, they no doubt put one and one together and came up with two people meeting on the sly.

Ute came to teach her final lesson at Babel. She thought everything would be all right now that Shelley was seeing Ross. Wayne gritted his teeth and slammed his office door again. Shelley turned scarlet, realizing Ute's implication; Shelley had fallen under Ross's spell, so he would encounter no more obstacles.

The engineers who had expected to study German at Babel called to schedule their lessons. Shelley had to regretfully inform them that she had just lost a German teacher and couldn't offer them the intensive work they'd discussed until she hired and trained someone else. They called back an hour later to say they would be learning German at Elite instead.

Shelley called Wayne into her office. He sat stonily in front of her while she delivered the bad news. She wanted to rage at him that it wasn't her fault this had happened. She'd done everything she could to keep Ute, everything she could to keep the client. Ross simply had more clout and flexibility than she did.

As Wayne rose to leave, Francesca informed her that Ross was on the telephone for her. The blistering contempt in Wayne's eyes burned her. Who had she been kidding? She and Ross couldn't separate business and pleasure. They lived in the real world, and no one would let them.

Ross, Ross, she cried silently. "Tell him I can't talk now, Francesca.

Tell him I'll call him back later."

"Are you sure?" Francesca asked with concern. "He should know what's happened to you —"

"Just tell him," Shelley ordered.

Ross called three more times that afternoon. She refused to talk to him every time. She couldn't seem to focus on anything. Her work kept blurring in front of her eyes as she suppressed tears of sorrow and frustration.

Finally she gave up and went home early. She didn't even bother to tell Wayne she was going. She couldn't face the accusing look in his eyes again today. Francesca's sympathetic concern was equally hard to bear when Shelley said goodbye.

Alone in her familiar, cozy apartment, she knew she'd have to call Ross and tell him they had to break it off. But she didn't have the strength to face him. Not now, not yet. Instead she gave in to the tears and cried her eyes out.

After her vagabond years, her job represented so much to her in terms of her self-esteem, her capabilities and her future. She felt almost maternal toward all her staff and clients. She took her responsibilities very seriously.

But then there was Ross, the most fascinating man she'd ever met. Certainly the most complex and confusing one, too: exciting, intelligent, evasive, tender, charming, exasperating, sexy, brave. No one like him would ever come her way again, and she'd regret it *forever* if she just passed him by.

She had wanted the job *and* the man, and had briefly kidded herself she could have both. But it was becoming eminently clear that she couldn't. And her practical nature told her that a bird in the hand was worth two in the bush. . . . He would leave eventually, anyhow. He never stayed in one place for long.

His leaving, however, would probably mean he had effectively finished off her career. So why not take him up on his offer, start a whole new career at Elite?

As Ross's girlfriend. As his paramour.

Maybe not. She really was good at her job. Henri Montpazier and the others would recognize that.

But she wasn't a quitter, damn it! And that's what she would be doing to Babel, her staff, and all her experience there if she left to go to Elite and Ross. She really would be the rat deserting the sinking ship. She would be going against everything she believed in, everything she'd ever been taught.

She just couldn't do it. But could she reject Ross? She decided with steely determination that she would have to.

The doorbell rang. Shelley frowned. Normally she would still be at work at this time of day. Who knew she was at home?

There was an impatient knock as Shelley wiped her tear-streaked face. She stood up and walked toward the front door sluggishly.

"Who is it?" she called huskily.

"Shelley, let me in," said Ross.

Eight

"*W*hat are you doing here?" Shelley asked.

"Open the door and I'll tell you," was the muffled reply.

"Ross, not now. I can't . . ." Her voice stopped as tears welled up in her eyes and spilled over her cheeks again.

"Let me in or I'll pick the lock, Shelley."

She choked on unexpected laughter. How like Ross, she thought. No traditional heavy-handed threats to bust down the door. She also had no doubt that he could indeed pick the lock. With a sigh and a reluctant smile, she let him in.

He pushed his way past her without an invitation and closed the door. His worried blue gaze took in her puffy eyes and tear-streaked face. He tried to put his arms around her. She backed away. He froze, then let his arms drop to his sides. She steeled herself against the hurt in his eyes, hurt he was trying to conceal from her.

"How did you know I was here?" she asked.

"Francesca told me."

"She — she —" Shelley sputtered.

"Relax. She didn't want to, I just convinced her to. When you wouldn't answer my calls, I," he paused, phrasing his words carefully, "I got worried. Everything seemed so good, so right between us last night, I couldn't believe you had changed your mind. So I went over to your office to see you. Wayne stomped off and slammed his door the minute he saw me. Not very subtle, is he? Francesca kept wringing her hands and babbling in Italian. So I got her to tell me what had happened and where you had gone."

"Oh."

His eyes raked her face. "I hate to see you cry," he said huskily. "I hate to be the cause of it."

She didn't deny that he was her number one pain. "If you know what happened . . . Ross, we just can't . . ."

"Be lovers?"

She nodded.

"The hell we can't," he said determinedly.

"Please, after today —"

"What's the very worst thing that could happen?" he challenged.

"I could lose my job in total disgrace because I'm sleeping with my competitor."

"Wrong. You could allow a bunch of men in New York and Chicago who don't really care about you to dictate your life and choose your friends for you."

"That's easy for you to say. You won't get into trouble over this!"

"Henri knows about us and he's furious," Ross corrected.

"How does he know?"

"I told him."

"You *told* him? Why, for God's sake?"

"Because I'm not ashamed of wanting you or afraid of what he'll do to me. And I don't want someone else to tell him first."

Shelley backed down for a moment. It had never even occurred to her to call Jerome herself and calmly explain that she was seeing Ross but wouldn't let it affect her work.

"Jerome would never buy it," she said aloud. "And Montpazier still won't fire you"

"That's true, Shelley. But if Babel fired you, you wouldn't be quitting, and perhaps then you could take my job offer with a clear conscience."

"I don't know," she said miserably.

"There's always an alternative if you want something badly enough. Or do you just not want me that much?"

She turned away from him, intimidated by the challenge in his voice. She suddenly had the feeling that he'd shown more courage than she, and she wasn't proud of that. She also didn't know what to do next, and that was unusual for her. He was turning her whole life upside down.

She heard the faint rustle of clothing and looked behind her. Ross had slipped off his jacket and was undoing his tie. She watched, wide-eyed, as he slid it out from under his collar and let it drop to the floor. He undid his cuff links and tossed them on the coffee table.

"What are you doing?" she whispered breathlessly.

"Consolidating my position."

"What?"

"Is that the bedroom through there?" His voice was gentle but determined.

"Ross, can we talk about this?" she asked faintly.

"I don't think so," he murmured, moving slowly toward her. His eyes, filled with a combination of desire and tenderness that drained her of common sense and clear thought, burned into her.

"Think about this first" Her voice was breathless with anticipation, telling him everything he needed to know.

He put his hands on her shoulders and drew her near, kneading the firm flesh of her arms in a seductive massage that made her feel limp yet curiously vibrant.

"I have thought about this. I've thought about it till it's driven me crazy," he murmured. "I thought of it the first moment I laid eyes on you, and it's been impossible to stop thinking about it ever since."

He lowered his mouth to hers slowly, just as slowly as he had the first time he'd ever kissed her. Sensing what he wanted, wanting to please him, she arched up toward him and met his lips with her own, showing him that he wasn't the only one who'd lain awake nights imagining this.

Their lips clung warmly, mouths melding, tongues mating, and Shelley was overwhelmed by how right it was, how absolutely destined she was to be held in his arms. She slid her hands into his luxuriant black hair and pressed her body tightly against his, wanting him to know how she, too, had longed for this.

In one graceful motion he scooped her up in his arms and, with a smooth, unhurried stride, headed unerringly toward the bedroom. How like a fantasy he was, she thought tenderly. No awkward moments, no clumsy movements. She wondered whether she could fulfill any of his fantasies. She hoped so.

He set her down beside her double bed and buried his hands in her coppery hair, pulling out the clips that held it up, stroking it, caressing it, inhaling its fragrance.

"I tried to stay away from you when you asked me to," he whispered. "I tried to pretend I could treat you lightly. I even tried not to think about you at all." His hands slid behind her and pulled down her zipper. "None of it worked for me, Shelley. Nothing will work for me but this." He took a shaky breath as he felt the warmth of her soft skin beneath the dress. "I don't know where this will lead, but I can't take the safe way out."

"No, I know you can't," she murmured lovingly, already pulling at the buttons of his shirt with trembling fingers. Of course he couldn't take the safe way out of their inconvenient mutual fascination any more than he could take the safe life offered by his wealthy family and privileged birth, or any more than he could take a safe path to maturity and manhood. She should have realized he would walk willfully into the eye of the storm, pulling her with him. "Thank you," she said suddenly.

"For what?" he asked, his breath catching as her hands slid inside his shirt to touch his hard chest.

"Thank you for not letting me be safe," she said irrationally. "Thank you for not letting me be sensible anymore."

He grinned, stroking her hair, caressing her bare back. He pressed a soft kiss to her forehead. "Oh, Shelley." His voice was tender, like his touch, like his lips, like his eyes, his blue, blue eyes. "Wait a minute," he gasped as she started to unfasten his belt.

"This was your idea," she reminded him.

"And it's a very good one. But there's one thing even we should be sensible about." She looked up at him questioningly, her eyes already dazed with passion. "I always think of everything, so I'm ashamed to admit that I rushed over here without . . . uh . . . preparing. And since I don't usually carry around . . . Stop laughing, I'm being serious," he chided.

"I really like it when you're not perfect," she said with delight. "Don't worry about it. I'm safe," she assured him.

"I'm so glad to hear that," he murmured, pulling her hips against his. "I'm in no condition to make a trip to the drugstore."

"Yes, I can tell."

"So, get on with what you were doing," he insisted, pulling her hands back to his belt buckle.

She offered her mouth up to his, willingly, generously, as her hands fumbled at his clothing. He pulled her dress over her head and looked at her standing there in her lacy underwear, her curly hair tumbling around her shoulders. How many times had he pictured her this way? How many times had he undressed her in his mind, imagining the milky smoothness of her skin, the lush fullness of her breasts straining against her bra, the mysterious swell and curve of her hips under those delicate panties?

Hot possessiveness flooded him, overwhelming and unfamiliar. He wanted her to be his, wanted to be the only man she undressed for ever again, the only man to see her gray eyes fill with warmth and desire as she slid the straps of her bra down her shoulders and stepped teasingly away from him. He had the disturbing feeling that he could kill another man for doing what he did as he pulled her closer and yanked her undergarments off with rough haste.

Shelley sighed exultantly as his hands slid over her body, touching her with obsessive longing, caressing her as if he owned her, handling her gently, roughly, intimately, without hesitation or apology.

She pushed his shirt from his shoulders. "Oh, Ross," she moaned with pleasure. Eager to enjoy the rest of him, she pushed his pants down his narrow hips. The heavy weight of his manhood, fully aroused, filled her questing hands, and she drew in a sharp breath, suddenly feeling hot and flushed all over.

"Don't stop there," he growled, pulling her hands away from his body and impatiently pushing his trousers farther down so he could kick them off.

She put her hands against his chest to hold him away from her so her eyes could travel admiringly over him. His body was smooth and hard, firm and muscular everywhere, powerful and well developed from the dangerous life he'd purposely chosen as a youth.

She sighed again and slid her arms around him, pressing herself close, pushing her plump breasts against his chest, knowing instinctively that it would excite him.

Ross heard an animal sound of hunger come from deep inside him and felt astonished by it as his arms slid convulsively around Shelley.

Slow, go slow, he reminded himself as he tumbled her onto the bed. Pleasure her, use some finesse, he thought as he pillaged her mouth, greedily drinking her kisses. He had learned to do this with skill and grace; he had asked women in a dozen countries to tell him what pleased them; he had always been breathlessly told he was an exquisite lover. And now, when it mattered most, when he was with the one woman he would gladly burn in hell to please, he seemed to have lost all control of himself.

Be gentle, she's so petite, a silent voice chided as his mouth moved roughly over her face. His hands squeezed her breasts, admiring her, worshipping her, unable to stop touching and kneading and enjoying her ripeness, her femininity, her softness.

Shelley groaned. He paused, using every fiber of strength to pull his sanity together. "I'm sorry," he said, the apology coming out as a choked murmur, the words barely distinguishable.

"Good," she moaned with difficulty. "It's so good. Oh, Ross. More. Please."

Her passionate plea tore through him, setting him on fire, silencing the voice of experience, teaching him to make love to her with blind instinct. Her mouth met his again, and her hands stroked him with the same rough passion he was feeling. She pulled away and nuzzled him affectionately, her warmth unlike anything he'd ever known.

He lowered his head to her breasts and suddenly felt her hands in his hair, pulling, tugging, stroking, telling him *yes, yes, let's try this now.* He reached up to hold one of her hands, feeling affection rush through him even as passion consumed him. With his other hand he kneaded one full breast while he nuzzled and kissed it. Shelley was murmuring to him, soft words of delight that he couldn't make out but could easily interpret.

He kissed the palm of her hand, the sweet tips of her breasts and the soft hollow between them. He ran his tongue around the pink areola of a tightly puckered nipple, then kissed it again. She panted, and the sudden rise and fall of her breasts drove him wild. He slid one knee between her legs and pressed it against the apex of her thighs, feeling the teasing silkiness of her pubic hair and the hot wetness it shielded.

"Please," Shelley murmured, not even sure what she was asking for. Only for it to continue, for it to go on, for him to keep touching her like this. She felt his mouth, hot and wet, slide across her breast and fasten around her nipple. The hand that held one of hers squeezed convulsively. She arched upward and pulled his head down, and she pushed her aching feminine core against his hard knee. She moaned and writhed against him and showed him without shame how much pleasure he was giving her.

He tugged at her nipple, his tongue rough, his teeth gentle, his lips tender. He let go of her hand to massage her other breast with firm, possessive strokes of increasing urgency. He changed his position so that his hips slid smoothly between her legs to let her feel his hard, throbbing desire for her pressing against her waiting flesh.

Shelley sobbed suddenly, unable to contain the feelings welling up inside her. She slid her hands down his back and dug her fingers into the hard, tense flesh of his buttocks. She ground her hips against him in silent urging.

His shaking hand found hers and guided her to him. "Show me where you want me to go. Put me inside you," he pleaded hoarsely.

She did, eagerly, wantonly, greedily rising to meet his first strong thrust. She was so small, so hot and tight, that he tried to enter her slowly, but she wouldn't let him. She arched toward him, relishing the sensations as he slid forcefully inside her body, pulling him deeper, wanting him to thrust into her very soul.

They established a fast, urgent rhythm immediately, perfectly attuned to each other. They writhed against each other, murmuring endearments and harsh compliments, their sweat-slick bodies gliding together and apart in perfect harmony, in and out, up and down.

"Deeper," she begged, *"deeper.* Harder. Oh! Oh, yes, yes . . . Like that . . ."

He was ferocious and tender at once, a demon lover, a dark angel. He was the lover she had never even imagined, too erotic for dreams, too earthy for fantasy. She shared every shred of her body and soul with him and felt him accept it with greedy delight and offer up his own in return.

"Hot, oh, Shelley, so hot, so . . . soft," he muttered hoarsely, his mouth moving roughly against her neck, his hands touching every part of her they could reach.

Suddenly she felt her whole body flooding with fire, desire giving over to satisfaction, earth giving way to heaven. "Oh, Ross, I'm . . . *Oh, Ross.*"

In the eye of the storm at last, she gave in to the luscious liquid feelings, melting and drowning in a long, wavy burst of pleasure that sent her mind spinning with the beauty of it and fed her body with everything it had ever hungered for. She felt him shudder and collapse on top of her, felt his heat pour into her as he trembled and harshly whispered her name, heard his long, ragged groan of masculine satisfaction.

Long, long minutes later, when his chest had stopped heaving and the world had stopped flying apart around the two of them, Ross pulled together what precious little strength he had left and rolled off her small frame, pulling her with him so that she rested against him. She curled around him and nuzzled him affectionately, a contented purring sound coming from deep inside her.

He smiled softly, feeling happier than he'd ever felt in his life. He had pleased her, he thought with thoroughly masculine delight. He had wanted nothing in life so much as to make her writhe and sob and purr with pleasure, and even so, he was astonished at how glad he was to have succeeded.

"You look smug," Shelley said lazily, too satisfied to sound critical.

He opened his eyes to find her looking up into his face. He realized that he had never shared with anyone the kind of intimacy he had just enjoyed with her. After what had just happened between them, he knew he'd never be able to hide anything from her again. He couldn't imagine even wanting to. So he let her see the open vulnerability in his heart, his astonished pleasure, his sweet satisfaction and, well, yes, his smug delight.

Her love-soft eyes darkened ever so slightly. "If you look at me like that, I'm going to make inappropriate demands," she warned.

He grinned. "Just try me," he challenged huskily.

She sighed and laid her head back on his shoulder. "In about an hour."

"Make it a half hour, and you've got a deal."

"You're such a braggart."

"*Tu m'inspires.*" He closed his eyes and savored the feel of her. Her tumbling hair covered his shoulder and tickled his chin, her smooth cheek rubbed absently against his chest, her breasts pressed against his ribs, her soft thigh rested intimately between his legs. Of their own volition, his hands started traveling over her with soft, caressing wonder, patiently discovering details he had missed in the fury of their passion.

Shelley sighed deeply, feeling a wonderful feminine satisfaction in knowing he couldn't keep his hands off her. The feeling was mutual, actually, and she lazily began exploring him, fascinated, enthralled, curious, fiercely proud of the body she only half realized she was swiftly starting to think of as her personal property.

"*J'adore tes cheveux . . . ta peau . . . tes seins . . . ton dos . . .*" he murmured absently, naming her parts as he explored them, loving everything he discovered. He was glad she understood French, since the words seemed more appropriate, more intimate in that language.

As their strength returned, their curiosity grew more insatiable. She sat up finally, wanting to see everything she'd been touching, wanting to see his face as they touched each other. He watched her with pleased, heavy-lidded eyes, studying her leisurely, languidly. His gaze slid below her waist and his eyes widened. Her thighs were slightly pink where he had lain between them, irritated from the friction between their over-heated bodies.

"Was I too rough?" he asked throatily.

"No." Her voice was certain, her smile positively feline. The cat that had gotten the cream. "It was . . ."

"Special," he finished for her. "Very, very special."

She nodded. He kissed her hand and held it against his cheek. He released it and traced an imaginary line down her breast, lightly stroking the nipple, which hardened instantly at his touch. In astonishment he realized his own body was already hardening in response, wanting her again, excited by her quick response to him, intrigued by her lush beauty.

"Come here," he said gruffly, pulling her down to the pillows.

She glanced down his body and her eyes sparkled with mischief and desire. "So you weren't bragging after all. Can I count on this all the time, or is this a special occasion?"

"I think you're to blame," he informed her.

"Hey, *guapo*, does this mean you're glad to see me?"

"*Ti voglio bene,*" he murmured.

"Is that one of the dozen phrases your friend once taught you for meeting Italian women?" she asked suspiciously.

"Uh-huh."

"That phrase is pretty specific, Ross. You must have made friends awfully quickly with the girls in Milan."

"I'm terribly charming," he reminded her, losing interest in the subject. "Do you like this? Ah, yes, I can see that you do."

"Oh . . . yes, I do. Your hands . . ."

"What about my hands?"

"They have no shame," she said in a strangled voice.

"Neither do my lips."

Shelley gasped as he proved his point. Suddenly she was breathing rapidly again, her body aching, her heart demanding, as if they hadn't just finished making love.

"Slow," he whispered against her hot flesh. "This time let's do it slowly."

"Yes," Shelley agreed breathlessly.

"And I want to watch you this time."

She nodded, suddenly unable to speak, unable to think, able only to feel and enjoy. She moaned pleadingly.

"Tell me what you want," he urged, a new intimacy, a new caring, in the request. .

"Like that . . . Just like . . ." A long time later she begged, *"Please."*

"What?"

"I want . . . you," she gasped.

"Inside you?"

"Yes!"

"Like this?" His tongue was hot and clever and bold.

"Ohh . . ." She trembled in a sudden, shattering climax. She felt him move against her, felt his fingers take the place of his tongue so he could watch her as he had said he wanted to. And, stunned at her own boldness, amazed at the wildness he stirred in her, she let him watch without shame as she accepted his gifts.

He kissed her tenderly after her body had quieted. *"Belle, comme tu es belle,"* he murmured, and she felt as beautiful as he said she was.

He rolled over on his back and pulled her on top of him. He grasped her hips, raised her in the air, and lowered her gently to his waiting body, arching his back as she wiggled to accommodate his size and hardness. He closed his eyes, fighting for control as she squirmed from side to side and pushed herself down until the curly reddish hair between her thighs met and mingled with the black hair between his.

She stilled at last, sitting above him, watching his face, savoring this moment of their union. He opened his eyes.

"Slowly," he reminded her in a passion-roughened voice.

She nodded, too full of tenderness and anticipation to answer him. They made love with exquisite, excruciating slowness, watching each other, relishing the pleasure they brought each other, stopping when they felt themselves approaching the edge, resting and then starting over again.

The sky darkened outside the window, but inside Shelley's bedroom, time came to a standstill. She didn't know how many times they stopped and started in their mating dance, how many times their bodies surged together in the irresistible rhythm of love, how many times they reached out to touch and fondle each other. They whispered to each other, giving and taking pleasure with frankness, with a total freedom that Ross had never known, with a lack of inhibition that Shelley had never imagined.

Their breath grew so harsh they could no longer speak. The sky grew so dark that they could no longer see each other's eyes. Shelley's body gleamed with perspiration in the moonlight, and Ross's chest was damp and hot. They finally reached a point where they couldn't wait, couldn't hold out, couldn't bear the fine torture of near-climax any longer, and they let the flood of soul-searing pleasure engulf them. Shelley cried out and collapsed against him, sobbing, letting him crush her in his arms as shudders racked his body. Wave after wave of fire washed through her, burning her to cinders, leaving nothing in its wake but exhaustion mingled with the greatest satisfaction she'd ever known.

"You're still in your robe," Ross said, entering the apartment later that evening. They had dozed and showered together, then he had gone home to pick up some clothes. Neither of them had questioned that he would spend the rest of the weekend at Shelley's apartment. She could barely stand to let him out of her sight for ten minutes, and the hotly possessive glitter in his eyes confirmed that he felt the same way.

"I saw no point in getting dressed," she informed him, "since you'll probably rip off my clothes and ravish me again as soon as I'm done feeding you."

"Hmm, very sensible, as usual. What are we eating?" He groaned when he saw the cardboard containers sitting on the kitchen table. "After the good time I've shown you tonight, couldn't you have done better than leftover Chinese?"

"It's not leftover. I just ordered it."

He frowned at her bathrobe. "How did you get this without getting dressed?"

"I had it delivered, of course."

"Did the delivery boy see you like this?" he demanded.

Shelley looked down at her thick, floor-length, terry-cloth robe with the ragged hem and sighed. "Relax. I'm not a picture of glamour and seduction in this thing, Ross."

"You are to me," he said.

"Get that look out of your eyes," she chided. "I'm starved." She turned away from him and started opening the cardboard containers. Ross slipped his arms around her.

"Humor me. Say something romantic."

"*Ta gueule.*"

"That's not romantic, it's downright rude," he chided.

"Moo goo gai pan."

He sighed. He slipped his hand inside the robe and caressed a soft, warm breast. Shelley sighed. "*I tuoi seni sono come due pesci,*" he said seductively.

Shelley burst out laughing. "Ross, are you sure that's what your Italian friend taught you to say?"

"Well, it's been a few years. What's so funny?"

"You just told me my breasts are like two fish."

He laughed. "Maybe that's why that line never worked for me."

"Sit down and eat, Romeo."

"Wait a minute. I came prepared this time."

"I told you I was already prepared," she teased him.

"No, I brought the important stuff this time." He pulled a bottle of expensive champagne out of the grocery bag he'd brought in with his overnight bag.

"This costs a fortune. You're so frivolous."

"But extremely well dressed."

"Hey, that reminds me. Since those dresses yesterday didn't cost me anything —"she batted her eyelashes at him " — I can afford something else. Can we go shopping tomorrow?"

He considered it as she started eating. "Only if it's a lingerie shop."

"That's so impractical, Ross. I don't need sexy underwear for work, and you've made it abundantly clear that I won't stay in it more than a minute or two around you."

"We'll negotiate tomorrow," he decided, digging into a carton of roast pork and vegetables.

They ate and cleaned up and talked and, surprised at how familiar they were already growing with each other, made love again.

They went shopping Saturday and compromised by going to several different shops. Ross bought her a sexy nightgown, which, as she had predicted, she only got to wear for a few moments before it wound up on the floor next to her bed. And that was in broad daylight. Before Ross she would have been scandalized at wasting so much time in bed. But with Ross the time was anything but wasted.

She showed him around some of her favorite places in Cincinnati, slipped her arm companionably through his as they walked through Sawyer Point, laughed as he screwed up his face while tasting some of the local brands of beer, and bickered with him about whether or not they'd eat Chinese food again that night.

The weekend passed in a haze of pleasure, both physical and emotional. It wasn't until late Sunday night that Shelley permitted herself to think about Babel. She left Ross sleeping the sleep of deep exhaustion after having made love to her yet again that day, and went into the kitchen to make a pot of coffee. She was sitting at the kitchen table when she felt her lover's familiar touch. He massaged her shoulders for a moment, then kissed the top of her head. His arms slid around her with easy grace.

"Two nights in your bed and already I can't sleep unless you're beside me," he murmured against her hair. He released her and slid into the chair across from hers. Their eyes met. "I woke up alone, and it didn't take a genius to figure out that you were in here brooding about work."

"I have to face it. I have to decide how I'm going to handle the job, my staff, my bosses . . . even you"

"You're a remarkable woman. No, don't interrupt. You have insight and perception and courage, and you'll know how to deal with each of them when the time comes." He touched her cheek, his gaze soft. If only she would resign and work with him, he thought. But she had cut him off the one time all weekend he'd suggested it again. "I would give anything for us not to be opponents. I would give anything not to complicate your life this way."

"Anything?" she teased halfheartedly. "You wouldn't even leave nicely on Friday when I asked you to."

"I've never been in this situation before, Shelley, and if I'm not as practical as you, I still knew all the reasons for avoiding you. I just couldn't do it."

He hadn't shaved, and the shadow of a beard darkening his cheeks made him look rakish and dangerous. As always she found his departure from perfection irresistibly appealing. His faith in her ability and his admission of his untamable desire for her added fuel to the bonfire burning inside her. She didn't want to make love, not right now; they just had. They had made love so many times this weekend that her whole body ached with a delicious pain of weariness and a sweet feeling of being well used.

No, something deep inside her craved something other than sex, something stronger, longer, deeper. She swallowed, emotion welling up in her and threatening to spill over as tears, tears that would confuse and concern him. Suddenly, without forethought, she stood up, rounded the table, and slid onto his lap.

He sensed something happening inside her. "What is it?" he whispered.

"Just hold me," she pleaded softly. "Hold me tight."

Unable to fathom her sudden change of mood, he did as she asked, wishing he could always shelter her as he was doing at this moment.

"You must be kidding!" Jerome said in obvious irritation.

"I wouldn't kid about this, Jerome," Shelley said quietly. "I tried to stop it, I tried — we tried — to stay apart. But we can't. If you insist I resign, then I will. I am aware that, despite my guarantees to the contrary, you may feel I can no longer —"

"Don't be ridiculous," Jerome snapped. "You know I don't want you to resign." There was a long silence on the telephone line. "I have to think about this, Shelley. This is really out of the blue. I'll call you back later, okay?"

Having broken the news to her immediate superior eased more of Shelley's tension than she would have guessed. She faced Wayne and Francesca with determination, feeling more confident than she had in quite a while. She was still the boss, after all. Wayne might have some legitimate objections to her situation, but he'd better behave maturely or she'd put him in his place.

To her surprise Wayne looked sheepish and embarrassed, not at all like the sullen, angry young man she'd expected to find. Francesca was still worried about the outcome of events, but she beamed and repeated Italian platitudes about love conquering all. Shelley decided not to speak to her teachers. Let them believe whatever they wanted to believe. She would be discreet, but she wouldn't sneak around, nor would she justify herself to anyone. Jerome finally called the office just as she was preparing to meet Ross for dinner. She braced herself for his decision, feeling proud of herself despite everything. Whatever happened she was behaving, under the circumstances, the way she had been raised to behave. Her parents would be proud of her if they knew. So would Ross, if only she could have told him.

"First of all," Jerome said as Shelley held the phone to her ear, "I want you to call me every single day to report professional developments. I will count on you to tell me the moment, the very moment, you feel your personal life is impeding your professional conduct. *If* that happens," he added gruffly.

"Okay," Shelley agreed.

"I will not tell anyone else about this, and neither will you, apart from those who already know."

"You don't want headquarters to know?" she asked cautiously.

"Are you kidding? Shelley, I've worked with you for, two years, I've respected you the whole time, and I like you personally. Therefore, I'm prepared to trust you. I'm willing to believe there's no immediate reason to fire or transfer you. But do you honestly think they would agree with me?"

"No, but what if —"

"You've reported the situation to your immediate superior and met your obligations. Any other action is my responsibility. So let me handle it as I see fit, Shelley."

"Okay, Jerome. And thank you," she added warmly.

Over dinner that night, she told Ross that she had handled it. She was dying to say more, to tell him how nervous she'd been, how sheepish Wayne seemed to feel, how sensibly she'd acted, how supportive Jerome was. But they had agreed not to talk about their jobs, and it was the best decision. She could not safely betray the shaky state of affairs in her school to Elite's boy genius. So she told him she had handled it, and left it at that.

Ross knew better than to press Shelley for details and he recognized that she was merely being practical. It was better to leave that door shut than to open it even a crack. But he was dissatisfied. He wanted to share his day with her and to hear about hers. How had she felt when she broke the news to her superior in Chicago? How had Wayne treated her today? Was the day full of unbearable tension, or had things returned to normal in her office?

He wanted to tell her his suspicions about one of the teachers at Elite. Evidence suggested that the teacher had stolen an abundance of teaching materials from Elite's storage room and was offering Elite teaching methods out of his home at half the price. He also wanted to share his dislike of Chuck's secretary with Shelley. There was no real reason to fire the woman, but he didn't trust her; Shelley might be able to offer him some insight if he told her about it. Instead he suggested they go to a movie after dinner.

The rest of the week followed much the same pattern. They met in the evening, after an entire day of looking forward to seeing each other. Though they experienced considerable strain over not being able to talk about their working day, they balanced it with all the other things they enjoyed talking about. Sometimes they made love in her apartment before going out, and other times they met in town. He ended every night in her bed, holding her, touching her, sometimes making love to her again, sometimes just enjoying the warm comfort of sleeping with her. He never invited her to his hotel. He was sick of hotels and their anonymous decor. Shelley's apartment was a real home, her home, and he felt content there.

One evening he suggested they go away for the weekend.

Shelley looked up from the food she was preparing in her kitchen. "Why?"

He shrugged. "I want to take you away from all this." He glanced at the baskets of dirty laundry next to the couch.

She smiled. She had talked him into taking the laundry to the basement and doing it while she made dinner. "You're procrastinating," she said knowingly.

"I'm building spiritual strength for the task at hand," he corrected.

"Where would we go?"

"I don't know, this is your turf. There must be some quiet little resort within a couple of hours."

"I don't know about that . . . But I've never been to Lexington."

"Lexington?" he repeated without enthusiasm.

"Well, we could visit some of the horse farms during the day. Maybe even drive down to the Kentucky Horse Park. I'd like that."

He shrugged. "Sounds fine to me. As long as it's out of town and we don't spend *all* our time looking at horses."

"I'll let you pick the hotel. And don't let your secretary do it; everyone in town will know we're going away for a dirty weekend."

"It'll be plenty dirty," he promised her, his eyes gleaming. "I'll take care of it."

"Good, now go take care of our laundry, Ross. I think it's scandalous that you actually pay someone to do yours most of the time."

He gave a martyred sigh and carried the laundry out the door, muttering about getting himself involved with a girl with such hopelessly inflexible working-class ethics.

Nine

"This fresh air is wiping me out," Shelley said as she stretched herself awake in their hotel room on Sunday morning.

"You're telling me," Ross replied with exaggerated disgust. "There I was in that big, king-sized bed, all ready for round three last night, and you were sleeping so soundly even my energetic ardor couldn't rouse you."

"Sorry, did I miss something?" she asked blandly.

"I can make up for it now," he offered gallantly.

"Mmm," Shelley sighed dreamily as he took her in his arms and nuzzled her throat. There was a discreet knock at the door. "What's that?"

He guided her hand. "Obviously that's my —"

"I mean that knock at the door," she chided.

"Oh." He rolled his eyes heavenward with a why-do-I-even-try look. "I suppose that's breakfast."

"Breakfast in bed? Oh, Ross, you are good to me. Let him in, I'm starved!" she exclaimed, slipping into her bathrobe.

They were staying at a small country inn outside of Lexington that Ross had chosen. Characteristically, it was elegant, charming, and extremely expensive. Seeing her dismay at the price tag, Ross had insisted he would pay and she had agreed that, yes, he certainly would.

Shelley uttered little sounds of delight as a sumptuous breakfast feast was laid out on a small table with elegant silver and linen. There was even a bottle of champagne to mix with the orange juice.

"Now where were we?" said Ross when they were once again alone. "Just about here, I think," he pulled her into his arms, "and I was about to —"

"Let's eat first. It'll boost your strength," she said, pulling away and sitting down eagerly at the table.

"I have plenty of strength left. Surely you noticed —"

"Yes, I couldn't help but notice. But I'm starved, Ross." She grinned with delight at his consternation. It was awfully nice to be wanted so badly by such a gorgeous man.

"You have no soul," he sighed, sitting down across from her.

"But plenty of appetite." Her look was full of promise as she added, "For all sorts of things."

Thus encouraged, Ross applied himself to breakfast. When they were done, he applied himself to Shelley.

"Hmmm," Shelley sighed as he pulled her down onto the bed. "Are you sure you're not using that aphrodisiac you read about in college? Your energy is quite remarkable."

"You're all the aphrodisiac I need," Ross said gallantly, loosening the belt of her bathrobe.

Shelley affectionately pushed his jet-black hair away from his forehead and stroked his cheek, tracing the beginnings of his five o'clock shadow.

"You look really sexy when you don't shave," she murmured.

"Right now, I *feel* really sexy," he confided.

"But Ross, we had agreed we would visit two more horse farms today. Daylight's burning." She rolled away from him and tried to hop off the bed. He grabbed her arm to keep her from getting very far away.

"I propose a change of itinerary," he said huskily.

"Now, Ross," she chided breathlessly. Her pulse raced as his eyes deepened to a dark, smoky blue.

"Face it, Shelley, when you've seen one multi-million dollar racing farm you've seen them all. Actually, after yesterday, I feel like we *have* seen them all."

"I thought that was the whole point of our trip down here," she said, letting him pull her a little closer.

"No, *this* was the whole point of our trip down here." He suddenly pulled her down into the pillows and kissed her lingeringly. "The horse farms were just something for you to tell Wayne and Francesca about when you get back."

Shelley grinned mischievously as she avoided another drugging kiss. "Then we'll have to see a few more to keep my cover story credible."

"Undercover work is my specialty. Get under the covers and leave everything to me," he whispered, pulling apart the front of her robe as she tried to slide away from him.

She gasped as his hands found her breasts. He touched her with the sureness of a familiar lover, knowing so well how to excite her. She wondered how it was possible that every time they made love it got better and better.

"Horse farms," she said weakly.

"Your heart's pounding, darling." He smiled as he slid his hands down her flat stomach. "Is the thought of wandering around a bunch of smelly stables that exciting?"

"Don't we have to check out of the room now?" she asked, rapidly losing interest in everything but him.

He kissed the soft hollow between her breasts. "I requested an extended check-out time."

"You did?" Shelley fumbled at the belt of his bathrobe.

"You should know by now that I always think of everything."

She pushed his robe off his shoulders then ran her hands across his back, loving the smooth play of his muscles as he shrugged out of the sleeves and then lifted her slightly to pull her robe out from underneath their entwined bodies.

"How much time do we have?" Shelley whispered against his lips.

He rolled over with her so they were closer to the bedside table. He peered at the clock. "About an hour." He arched a brow inquisitively as he looked down at her. "Think it'll be enough time?"

"If it's not, *I'm* not paying for another day in this room," she warned him.

"In that case . . ." he began suggestively, his hands sliding down her body to draw her thighs around him.

"We'd better get down to business," she finished for him.

Closing her eyes, Shelley pulled his face down to hers and kissed him lingeringly, opening her warm mouth to his questing tongue, clinging to him as passion chased away their teasing mood for more serious matters.

She arched her back and pushed her hips up to meet his thrusting entry into her body, welcoming him both physically and emotionally.

"Open your eyes. Look at me," Ross pleaded softly.

She did as he asked, wanting to please him in every way possible. The tenderness and vulnerability in his eyes swept through her, making her feel more womanly than she'd ever felt before. With their gazes locked and their bodies joined, she felt some powerful emotion pour through her. It was too strong for words, and she expressed it naturally, in the only way she could, by tightening her arms around his back, her legs around his hips, her softness around his hardness.

Ross shuddered and kissed her roughly. They moved against each other with a slow, burning intensity that robbed Shelley of breath or speech or thought. Her breasts were pressed so tightly against his chest that the labored rhythm of his breath became her own. Through the swirling fire of her passion she could hear fast ragged breathing and soft moans of pleasure, but Ross had become so much a part of her that she didn't know which sounds belonged to whom. She knew only that their pleasure was shared, mutual, and ever soaring, lifting them both to a higher plain before shattering their souls and letting them drift back down, softly, slowly, to return to the sweet weariness of their entwined bodies on a sun-soaked bed.

"Shelley?" Ross murmured a long time later, stroking her hair, as she lay curled against him.

"Hmmm?"

"We should get dressed," he said reluctantly, unwilling to give up the special warmth of afterglow he always felt in her arms.

She rubbed her face against him and inhaled deeply. "Five more minutes," she mumbled, tightening her arms around him.

He smiled slightly and kissed the top of her head. "Have I ever denied you anything?"

Tired as she was, Shelley found the strength to pinch him.

"Can I drive?" Shelley asked hopefully as they put their luggage in the Porsche that afternoon.

"Of course." She'd confessed her fantasies about the car to him, and he was glad to be able to make them come true for her. He wanted to make everything she'd ever dreamed of come true. But in their current position he was the man who would destroy some of her dreams. She was a woman of generous spirit, but he wasn't certain she could forgive him for that. He was growing increasingly certain he would never forgive himself for it. So, what was he going to do about it? There was always an alternative if one wanted something badly enough, he reminded himself. In this moment he wanted her most of all.

"I had a wonderful time this weekend, Ross," she said softly before starting the engine.

"So did I, darling." He kissed her cheek and admitted, "I even liked the horse farms. All of them," he added wearily.

"Thanks for humoring me yesterday. It was something I've wanted to do ever since I came to Cincinnati."

"I wasn't humoring you. *This* is humoring you," he said as she stomped on the brake suddenly to avoid hitting a tractor. "I had fun, anyhow."

"Where did you learn so much about horses? You can let your breath out, Ross, I see the Stop sign."

"My family had horses, here and in France."

"Oh. Do you visit your family much?" she asked curiously.

"When I can. I'd like to see some of them more than I do. I'm always moving around so much."

"Yes," she said hollowly, feeling the weight of that sudden reminder. She couldn't imagine her life once he'd left and gone off to some other city. "Ross . . ." she began hesitantly.

"Yes?" He wondered whether she, too, couldn't bear the thought of their living apart. His mind was already working on possible solutions to that problem.

"I read that you disappeared from Elite for about six months last year. No reason why, no knowledge of your whereabouts."

"That's comforting," he said dryly. "I didn't broadcast my reasons."

"Why did you quit? Only the truth," she added.

"I was tired. It's really that simple. Henri has always rewarded me well for the work I do. I had made enough money to give up work and just live on investments. I was tired of continent-hopping and sleeping in hotels and firing people and having no roots. I was exhausted, depressed, short-tempered. I quit. Henri asked me to consider it a leave of absence and to come back to work for him when I felt better. I refused because . . . because that seemed like a safe way out."

Shelley nodded, instinctively understanding a decision in him that she would have regarded as impractical in herself. "So where did you go?"

"I bought a seventeenth-century farmhouse and some land in Provence."

Shelley glanced at him in surprise. "You really did mean to settle down then?"

"Absolutely. I just wanted to live simply."

"And were you happy?"

"For a while. I renovated the house myself. It's a fabulous place, and it wasn't in bad shape really, but the work gave me great satisfaction. It seemed positive and productive. And it was tiring in a healthy way. I was glad to be near my family there. I enjoyed the slow pace, the simplicity. If I got bored, it was an easy drive to Nice. I had time to read books I'd been putting aside for years, time to think about my life and my past and put some perspective into it. It was very good for me."

"So, why did you leave and go back to Elite?"

He frowned thoughtfully before replying slowly, "Once my battle fatigue wore off, I discovered that I liked to work for a living and missed it. I could have been one of the idle rich merely by living off my trust fund and coaxing an allowance out of my mother; I realized I had never done that because I *wanted* to work. The farmhouse stopped seeming peaceful and started seeming pointless." He shrugged. "I decided to go back to work. I considered all my options, which were considerably broader than they had been when I'd first won my job from Henri in a poker game. But there was nothing that suited me as well as my job with Elite. It gives me more scope and freedom than anything else I could do, and it's always interesting and challenging. And, as a line of work, I like the language schools. It's a very people-oriented business."

"Hmm," Shelley agreed. "Henri must have been very glad to have you back."

"He was. At the risk of sounding immodest —"

"Who, you?"

"I'm the best at what I do. And he's very fond of me personally. He was hurt when I said I wanted to quit and nagged me incessantly to come back."

"I'm not surprised," she murmured. She, too, would be hurt when Ross left and would long for his return.

They were silent for most of the rest of the drive, each lost in thought. As they neared Cincinnati, Ross said, "Would it be entering forbidden territory to ask what future you would like for yourself at Babel?"

"I don't mind. I like running the school. I'd like to be promoted so I could operate with less of a stranglehold. Eventually I'd like to go to a bigger school with more challenges and a more diversified clientele. Sometimes I think I'd like to have one of the administrative jobs, because I think I could do a better job than the people doing it now. However, I like my day-to-day dealings with people, so I think I'm probably happiest as a school director."

"Hmm," Ross said absently, and for once Shelley wondered whether he'd been listening to her. They were both silent again until they reached her apartment.

Shelley parked the car near her building. Ross pulled her small suitcase out of the car and carried it up to her apartment for her. She made a pot of coffee and offered him some.

"Let's have it on the balcony," he suggested.

It was a small balcony, but the view was lovely. Shelley had once fantasized about sipping coffee out there on a Sunday afternoon with an exciting man. She wondered whether Ross knew. How like him to make her fantasies spring to life.

After a pleasant interlude on the balcony, he stood up. He met her questioning eyes. "I've got to go. I've got a lot of phone calls to make."

"You can use my phone," she offered, reluctant to see him leave.

"Business calls, Shelley."

"Oh. I see." She stood up.

"But it won't take more than a few hours. Why don't you take a long hot bath. . . ?"

"Uh-huh," she said, her interest perking.

"And get into that sexy little black dress I bought for you . . ."

"Uh-huh."

"And I'll be by at about eight o'clock to slow you what I had in mind when I talked you into getting it."

"I'll be ready, willing and waiting," she murmured against his lips as his strong hands massaged her back. She burrowed against him, loving the hard feel of his body, the musky smell of his skin, the way his smooth voice vibrated deep inside his chest.

It was only after he had left that she wondered what business he could possibly be taking care of on a Sunday afternoon. Something important was brewing. She tried to quell the sense of dread rising inside her. It was silly, since it had no basis in fact. But it wouldn't go away.

Ross showed up at eight o'clock, looking elegant and quite devastating in his evening attire. His comments about her appearance made her insides melt, and she suggested they just stay home and explore his theories. He grinned wickedly and said anticipation would create the necessary conditions for their experiment later this evening. Besides, he added, she would hospitalize him if she kept making so many demands on him. She reminded him in graphic detail just how unfair that accusation was.

He took her to a special performance given by the Cincinnati Symphony Orchestra for a particular charity that night. Afterwards they ate a very late dinner at an elegant restaurant.

"I'm getting so spoiled," she confessed. "Before I knew you, men usually took me out for pizza and a movie if it was a special occasion."

"Before I knew you, no one forced me to do laundry or eat reheated Chinese carry-outs."

"It's been a broadening relationship for both of us."

She talked him into taking her back to his hotel suite. She was surprised by his acquiescence, actually, since he had always been adamant about preferring her apartment. She'd insisted that they were too well dressed to end the evening in her cluttered little apartment, and he had good-naturedly agreed.

His hotel room was as spacious and luxurious as she had expected, based on the hotel's reputation. Ross dimmed the lights and swept her up in his arms, telling her the suite wasn't what he had brought her here to admire. He carried her to the bed, and there she discovered all the potential he had seen in her little black dress when he bought it.

With slow-burning sensuality he pulled the straps down her shoulders and hiked the skirt up around her waist. Later, when she was moaning and tearing at his clothes, he unzipped the dress and pulled down her silky panties.

Shelley woke up hours later, disoriented at first, since she was lying diagonally across a strange bed in a strange room. She recognized the weight on her stomach as Ross's head. One heavy arm was slung across her legs, and he lay naked above the covers, sleeping peacefully after the turmoil of their passion. The uncomfortable stricture around her middle was her black silk dress, now bunched around her waist in a thick, wrinkled band.

She closed her eyes, astonished at how wild he had made her, at how she had begged and demanded and devoured. She took a deep breath, straining against the weight of Ross's head and the silk band around her waist. Tonight had been another fantasy, one of his perhaps, since her imagination had never before conjured up some of the things they'd done together in this bed. Like all the moments she had known with him, however, it was too earthy, too real, for fantasy. It was love.

The thought surprised her at first, then blossomed into certainty. She glanced down at his sleeping face, his features pressed trustingly against her body. He was a magnificent lover and a fascinating man, true, but she could never have abandoned herself to him the way she had done tonight if she hadn't been in love with him.

She smiled wryly. In love with Ross Tanner. And she hadn't even known it till this moment. She should have realized. She had taken so many risks to be with him, had demanded so much of him, and offered so much in return, more than she had ever thought to offer to another human being. She was pressured every moment at work and enthralled by every moment in Ross's company, so she hadn't even stopped the whirlwind long enough to realize why she was doing all this.

Of course, this complicated matters dreadfully. But for now all she could do was bask in the warm knowledge that she had found the one man in all the world that she was meant to love, and that she was lying in his arms the moment she realized it. She stroked his dark hair, lightly so she wouldn't disturb his sleep, and dwelt on all the wonderful, fascinating, exasperating qualities that made up the man she loved.

And Ross? Did he love her? she wondered suddenly. He adored her; he had said as much, and she knew instinctively that he was more honest with her than he had ever been with anyone in his life. But he was a complicated man, and she didn't know how deep his feelings for her ran. She also didn't know what love meant to him and what he would want out of it.

His story about his time in Provence had told her one thing: he wasn't the settling-down type. He'd recognized the pleasures of a settled existence and had made a good effort at it, but he'd become restless and dissatisfied within six months. He had returned to his globe-hopping life at Elite, the job to which he said he was best suited. Where did a woman fit into all that?

He wanted to install her at Elite. Maybe in his mind that was as close to marrying her as he could come. Or maybe he just figured his infatuation for her would wear off when it was time for him to move on. Always one for the direct approach, Shelley nevertheless didn't think she could ask him a straight question about all this. She could be too hurt by the wrong answers.

She sighed, slowly returning to reality. She was in love with the man from Elite, but she was still the director of Babel. She was a woman of commitments, and despite her feelings, her only definite commitment was still to her job.

"Oh, my God," she said suddenly, realizing that the sky was starting to lighten. Her job! She couldn't leave Ross's hotel room and go to work in a little black silk dress. Especially not one in this condition. "Ross, wake up," she whispered urgently.

"Hmm?" He grunted sleepily, and burrowed against her side.

"Wake up. You've got to take me home," she insisted, struggling to sit up.

It took considerable determination and a little ruthlessness, but she finally got Ross awake enough to get dressed, help her straighten her dress and drive her home. When they reached her apartment, she told him they could probably still grab another hour or so of sleep if he wanted to come upstairs.

"No thanks, honey," he said groggily, running a hand over his unshaven face. "The day has already started in Europe, and I have a lot of calls to make there."

As was their custom, they didn't have any contact during the business day. Shelley wondered from time to time what Ross was up to with all these calls to Europe. Memories of their night together flashed through her mind at totally inappropriate moments, and she could feel her body stir. Her imagination was becoming awfully fertile. She was eager to tell him how special their lovemaking had been for her; last night she had fallen asleep immediately afterward in total exhaustion, and this morning she had nagged him to take her home. He was so tolerant, she thought fondly. She cherished her love for him like a delicious secret.

She would tell him she loved him, of course. She didn't know when or how, but whether he loved her or not, he should know that someone thought so highly of him that she had fallen in love with him. It would be her gift to him, whatever happened. But for now it was her secret and her comfort.

That was just about her only comfort that Monday. An old and profitable client told Shelley that they had decided to meet with Elite before renewing their contract with Babel. She overheard another client, a woman, telling Francesca that she had met that Mr. Ross Tanner and he was such a charming man, and so handsome it could make a woman think twice about her marriage vows!

Shelley gritted her teeth, trying not to let a very understandable resentment spoil her inner happiness or her erotic memories of the night before. But why did he have to be so very, very good at this?

She sighed, knowing she wouldn't respect him so much if he weren't so good at his job. She frowned suddenly. And could he respect her, when he was so much better at their profession than she? The thought troubled her, since she wanted his respect, had always wanted it. And though he had assured her a number of times that she had it, how could it continue if he wiped her out so easily?

Having wrestled with these thoughts all day, and having broken the news to Jerome about another regular client considering Elite, Shelley was feeling frustrated and tense by the time she met Ross in her apartment. His exuberance, his cheerful smile, his irrepressible good mood annoyed her unreasonably.

"I thought about last night all day today," he told her, his voice low, his eyes intimate. He brushed his lips across hers, and her response to him was so immediate, so uncontrollable, that she felt alarmed by it. She pulled back instantly, suddenly resenting the vulnerability he created in her.

"Is something wrong?" he asked, a concerned frown creasing his brow.

"No, I'm just tired."

He grinned seductively. "I can believe that. After the way you —"

"Can we eat out?" she interrupted suddenly. She didn't know why, but she had the sudden feeling that talking about last night would make her cry.

"Sure," he said, studying her, aware that she was shutting him out. Had something gone wrong at work? He knew better than to ask.

Their time together usually flew by, yet tonight dinner at Shelley's favorite Chinese restaurant seemed to drag by. Shelley picked at her food, which was unusual for her. Ross kept trying to draw her into conversation, but she didn't respond with her usual enthusiasm. He grew increasingly concerned, unwilling to let her bear her trouble alone, whatever it was.

"I don't want to talk about it," she snapped at him when he prodded her. His eyes widened. She was sometimes impatient with him, but never curt. She sighed. "I'm sorry."

"Did something happen at work? Is that it?"

She shrugged. It was work, and it was him. She loved and respected him, and she didn't know whether he could respect her if she kept losing out to him. She didn't know whether he could love her at all. She didn't know how long he'd be around, or that he ever even thought about such things. Since they had agreed not to talk about a very important area of their lives, they had left a lot of important things unsaid, despite their undeniable intimacy.

She was in love with him, and suddenly this carefully defined relationship with its uncertain future wasn't enough. Couldn't he see that? she thought with rising irritation.

They drove back to her apartment in tense silence. There had never been tension between them before, she thought sadly. She knew it was her fault, and she was miserably aware that she couldn't help it. She was tearing herself apart inside.

Ross glanced briefly at her in the dark car. He couldn't stand the doubts nagging at him. He felt all the hurt and despair of a rejected lover. Could her unfamiliar mood be due to last night? he wondered wildly. They usually cuddled and talked after making love, but she had fallen asleep instantly last night — or at least appeared to. This morning she had nagged him and seemed irritable, but in her usual chattery way — nothing out of the ordinary.

However, he'd have to be a fool not to realize that she had maneuvered him into a restaurant this evening specifically to avoid being alone with him, to avoid talking about last night. He'd been too exhausted last night and too groggy this morning to take a really good look at her. And now the restless, unhappy look in her eyes and the tired slump of her shoulders tore at his heart.

Had he been so satisfied, so completely fulfilled by their wild lovemaking that he'd failed to notice that she was disturbed? She was so sensual by nature, always so eager for him, always so uninhibited in his arms, always so delightfully greedy for more, that he couldn't believe the depth of what they'd shared last night had shocked or embarrassed her.

They were so close last night, so completely involved in each other, that their passion had reached a new level, a new depth. A new kind of trust and openness had blossomed between them, making their experience together richer than anything that had gone before.

Inflamed by their passion, plundering the depths of her body, sharing the secrets of his soul with her, giving all the dark passion and hidden vulnerability that was in him as well as the strength and joy and confidence, she became, somewhere in the midst of her sighs and cries and demands, the answer to every longing he'd ever known.

He couldn't give her up, he thought with fierce determination, and he couldn't let her slip away. In that hotel room in Kentucky this weekend, he'd discovered why all other hotel rooms had always seemed so lonely. The answer was obvious: Shelley wasn't in them. It was even the reason his lovely farmhouse in Provence had seemed barren, despite the care he'd put into it.

This weekend he'd finally understood what he needed: Shelley, everywhere, in every part of his life, forever and ever. And that was clearly impossible in Cincinnati. He had already taken considerable steps in the past two days to change their situation. He was taking a big gamble, just to be with her, he thought, suddenly feeling a little irritable himself. If only she wasn't so stubborn about her values!

He parked the car and turned to her in the dim lamplight. His heart went out to her and dampened his annoyance. She looked more miserable than he'd ever seen her.

"Shelley . . ." He wondered whether she'd want him to promise he'd never make love to her like that again. He didn't know that he could; all day he'd thought about making love to her like that again. He looked at her again and suddenly knew he'd do anything for her, even promise never to touch her again if it was what she wanted. "Shelley, last night we . . . were pretty wild."

"Uh-huh."

"Did I hurt you?"

"No, of course not," she said.

Ross suddenly had the feeling he might be on the wrong track but he pressed on. "Were you upset by what we did together?"

"No, Ross." Really, she thought, this was no time for him to be asking her to cater to his masculine ego. "In fact, I believe I kept telling you all the while that it was incredible, delicious, wonderful, the best thing that ever happened to me. . . . You can probably remember the rest."

He blinked. Her voice was impatient, even patronizing. He sighed with relief to realize that whatever was bugging her, it wasn't last night. He frowned in the next second. "Then what the hell is wrong with you?" he demanded, all tenderness going out of his voice.

She gaped at him in astonishment. "Wait a minute! You honestly thought that the reason I'm . . . not myself tonight is because I couldn't handle last night? Because you shocked my tender sensibilities? After everything we've done together, you honestly think I'm prudish or neurotic?"

"No, of course not, but —"

"Sometimes," she said in exasperation, "you're as dense as any man I've ever met. Can you really believe a woman acts the way I did last night and then spends all the next day feeling regrets?"

"No, I don't. But what else is different between us? You're not mad at the world in general. You're mad at *me* tonight, and I don't know why!"

There was a long silence before Shelley said, "I guess we're having our first fight." Would this be what ended their affair? she wondered.

"I guess we are," he agreed wearily. "Let's go upstairs. This may take too long to finish in the car."

"No."

"What do you mean, 'no'?" he demanded.

She took a deep breath. "I know I'm not being reasonable —"

"That's one thing we can agree on."

"I think I need some time alone to . . . think about things."

"What things?" he prodded.

"Come on, Ross. We're not a normal couple who met through friends or something. We have to deal with what other couples deal with, plus our professional situation and . . . and . . ." Tears started to spill down her cheeks, surprising them both. "Oh, my God," she said brokenly.

All his anger fled as he slid his arms around her and pulled her against him. She had always seemed so stable that he hadn't realized how strongly she felt the pressure. The sooner he put his plans into action, the better for both of them.

"Shelley, Shelley, I'm sorry, darling. I've been so selfish. I thought just because I was happy, you must be, too," he murmured soothingly. "I know it's been tough on you." He had found everything he needed in their relationship, but maybe she hadn't, he thought with a sudden lack of confidence.

She sobbed against his chest. How could he be happy? From nine to five he had to pretend she didn't exist, except as a competitor to be eliminated. She had to get some perspective, had to calm down. Oh, Ross, she thought, I love you too much.

"Come on, let's go inside," he said softly.

She shook her head. "I still want to be alone for a while. We'll talk about it tomorrow night, okay?"

"We can't. I have to go overseas tomorrow."

"You do?"

He nodded.

"How long?"

"Just a few days, darling. I'll be back by Friday." He waited.

"Then I'll see you Friday."

"Shelley . . ."

"Goodnight, Ross," she said huskily, and got out of the car.

"Shelley, this is Mike Paige at Keene International."

"Hi, Mike. What can I do for you?" Shelley said into the receiver.

She sat red-eyed and dispirited at her desk. A sleepless night of worrying and fretting had produced no positive results. She was in love with Ross whether she liked it or not, and she was still committed to her job whether she liked it or not. And everything else was as disturbing and as unresolved as it had been last night. Now she just wished for his safe return from wherever he'd gone. His absence was more painful than anything that had gone before. Is this what it would be like when he moved on to a new city eventually?

"Shelley, my boss has decided to sign with Elite."

She was silent. She felt as if someone had tolled her death knell at Babel.

"I'm sorry, Shelley. I wanted to go with Babel, but the final choice is his. He met with Tanner yesterday —"

"Ross met with him yesterday?" she interrupted suddenly.

"Yes, and offered a final contract which met all our demands . . ."

Mike continued talking, but Shelley scarcely heard another word. All she could think of was Ross. He had taken her away for the weekend, chased her around the horse farms, made devastatingly intimate love to her in his hotel room, slept in her arms . . . and then he got up and clinched a deal he knew she'd been after for months. Last night he had talked to her, held her, and soothed her, all the while knowing he had lowered the boom on her career. What did he think she was, some piece of skirt he could play with in the evenings? Didn't he know her career was as consequential to her as his was to him? Had he no respect whatsoever for her?

After the call was over she raged silently, pacing around the school. Wayne and Francesca looked at her warily, wondering what had caused her caged-tiger act.

How could he have behaved this way? How could he sleep in her bed every night while he spent every day wrecking her business? What kind of thoroughly selfish, amoral, thoughtless bastard was he?

Nothing would quiet her anger. She called Jerome to tell him she had lost the contract with Keene. She also told him that her relationship with Ross Tanner was over. How could she ever have been fool enough to make herself vulnerable to him? The man had no soul. Wayne, with his exaggerations, had been right about Ross all along.

Wednesday brought no relief to her wounded heart or her shattered self-esteem. She longed for Ross's return, but this time she longed to see his eyes when she told him to go to hell. She had never felt this way in her whole life and scarcely recognized herself. But then no one had ever betrayed and hurt her as Ross had.

On Thursday a special delivery letter arrived from headquarters. Of course, Jerome had had to tell them Shelley had lost the contract. Never mind that she had repeatedly asked for more bargaining tools. They would punish her now.

The letter was terse and to the point. They were extremely disappointed that she'd lost such an important contract to a competitor who'd only been in town for a few weeks. Considering Tanner's reputation, they would give her the benefit of the doubt and would neither demote nor fire her. However, they were considering moving her to a quieter location and replacing her in Cincinnati with someone who was more of a match for Ross Tanner.

Shelley's rage reached the breaking point. She picked up her mug of coffee and threw it across the room. Francesca knocked discreetly at the door and braved Shelley's wrath to come in and comfort her friend.

Once she had heard the whole story about Keene and Ross, Francesca took a long look at the letter from headquarters. "It is very insulting," she agreed. "And 'quiet location' probably means Outer Mongolia."

"How could he?"

"Ross?"

"Yes!"

"He never told you he was doing this?"

"No, of course not! We . . . I had decided that we should never talk about business."

"Then how could he tell you?"

"I . . . He couldn't, I guess. But how could he do this?"

"Shelley, at the risk of defending this man you have condemned to everlasting hell, how could he not do it? It is his job."

"It's my job, too!"

"Which is why you did your best to get that contract. You yourself have assured us all that you would not allow your relationship with this man to compromise your integrity. Would you expect less of him?"

"That's not fair!"

"It is only unfair, Shelley, because the answer is more difficult than you would like it to be. It is so of all human things."

Shelley sighed and sank into her chair. Maybe Francesca was right. Maybe Ross had to do this or he wouldn't be the man she loved. Maybe she was so angry because she had seen this moment approaching for days now, and the tension had overwhelmed her.

"What am I going to do?" she muttered.

"What do you want to do?"

"I want to kill Ross." She ran a hand through her tangle of coppery hair. "I want to turn back the clock and get that contract away from him."

"You may not need to turn back the clock."

"What do you mean?" Shelley asked, peering at her.

"He is out of town, *vero?* Overseas, yes?"

"Yes, probably gloating to Henri Montpazier in Paris about having wrapped up Cincinnati."

"But then he has not yet signed this contract with them. He has perhaps assumed they will sign it, but that is different."

"Yes, I suppose it is," Shelley said slowly.

"So, until tomorrow when he returns, you can try again. A last-ditch effort, I think you call it."

"Yes," Shelley said, frowning with concentration. "Your father . . .

used to go ahead and do whatever was necessary."

"Yes," said Francesca, following Shelley's train of thought. "And after all, Shelley, though this isn't Calabria, what else can headquarters do to you? Firing you would make little difference in a company that has shown so little support for you."

"Oh, Francesca, what would I do without you?"

"Hopefully, we will not have to find out."

Shelley called Mike Paige and told him to arrange a conference between himself, his boss, and herself for that very afternoon. She used every argument, every shred of charm, every bit of strength she had to accomplish just that much. Then she and Wayne set about writing a proposal that no one could beat, not even Ross.

"Headquarters will ax us both for this," Wayne warned her.

"Then why are you helping?"

"You're my boss. They're just a bunch of faceless men in New York."

"I'll take you with me to my one-room outpost in northern Alaska when I'm transferred," she promised.

"Forget it. I want a career with Elite. Have you seen the car Tanner drives? Well . . . I guess you have."

Since Mike Paige preferred Shelley to Ross, he was easy to convince. His boss was another matter. Not only was Shelley a mere woman, and a short one at that, but he had already made his decision and was as inflexible as granite. She really didn't think she could do it, but she used all the powers of persuasion she possessed. Her career at Babel, she realized, was shot to hell no matter what happened. Something more important than her career rested on this. Her self-esteem, self-confidence and self-respect hung in the balance. Most of all, the next time she faced Ross, she wanted to face him as an equal, not as someone whom he had beaten without effort, not as his weaker adversary.

She stumbled back to Babel late that afternoon. Wayne and Francesca were waiting for her.

"Well?" Wayne demanded the moment she entered the lobby.

She indulged in one moment of breathless suspense, then smiled triumphantly. "I got it!"

They hooted and jumped around in celebration. Teachers and students peeked out into the hallway to ask what the commotion was about. Shelley felt the greatest sense of victory she'd ever known as she showed Francesca and Wayne the signatures on the contract she'd prepared. It was hers, all hers.

She glanced at her watch. "The Chicago office is still open," she said. "I'm calling Jerome."

"He'll kill us," Wayne groaned.

"Ironic, isn't it? I don't have to tell him you —"

"Tell him. I'm Elite-bound. As soon as Tanner gets back into town.

Everyone knows the books over there are a hopeless mess."

"Maybe I'll even take that job as director he's always offering me." Shelley winked at Francesca.

"It's a shame they already have a secretary . . ." Francesca murmured.

Jerome was understandably stunned by her news. And full of questions. He blanched at the concessions she'd offered Keene and asked whether there was any chance of getting out of the contract.

"Oh, no, I'm afraid not, Jerome. It's all perfectly legal, signed, sealed, and delivered. Until the day they fire me, I *do* have the power to commit the school to contracts."

He was so eager to call New York that he didn't even bother to reprimand her. Nothing like this had ever happened at Babel before, and he didn't know what to do about it.

Shelley, Wayne, and Francesca went out to dinner that night, all feeling quite pleased with themselves. Shelley wondered why she had fretted so long over her responsibilities to Babel. The first time something went wrong, they'd been eager enough to forget about their commitment to *her*. And she was good, God, she was good! She had matched Ross Tanner, for goodness' sake, so they could just go eat crow!

The phone wouldn't stop ringing the next morning. Keene phoned a dozen times. Having delayed their decision for so long, they were now eager to get things under way. Jerome phoned to tell Shelley she had the surprise of her life coming to her; headquarters would call her in a few minutes. When the call came, Francesca and Wayne sat in Shelley's office, unblinkingly watching every expression on her face, straining to catch the voice of the national director of Babel in the U.S.

Shelley put down the receiver after only a few moments, a stunned look on her face.

"Well?" Wayne prodded. "Will we be hung or guillotined?"

"Neither. We're both being promoted."

"What?"

"They're . . . a little worried about my impetuousness, but just as pleased as punch that we took the contract right out from under Ross's nose."

Wayne digested this in silence for a while before saying, "What are we being promoted to?"

"You're to become assistant to the regional accountant in Chicago."

"Wow! I'm on my way! And you?"

"I'm to consolidate our position here until we know Ross's plans for Elite, and then I'm taking over a school twice this size in San Diego." She shook her head. "I can't believe this. I can't believe them."

"When do I leave? When do you get your raise? Who'll take over the books here?"

"I don't know. He just broke the news and said we'd receive everything in writing on Monday."

"Wow!" Wayne said again.

Things didn't slow down after that. New York called her little Cincinnati school more times that day than in the whole of her career there. They were full of questions, recommendations, and comments and, above all, congratulations. Shelley smiled wryly and took it all with a grain of salt. The sudden approbation of people who had condemned her only a few days ago left her unimpressed.

Ross was right. The worst thing that could happen was that she could let a bunch of men in New York who didn't care about her choose her friends. She was a good employee, but her first commitment had to be to her heart. And her heart was with Ross.

The phone rang. Francesca was making coffee for the afternoon students, so Shelley answered it. "Babel Language Center, can I help you?"

"Shelley, this is Ross. I'm at your place, I let myself in with the key you gave me. Any chance of your getting away early so we can talk? I have so much to tell you. And ask you."

"Ross . . ." She was so glad to hear his voice! "Ross. I'm furious with you! But that's okay, because I'm pretty sure you're going to be furious with me."

"What?"

"I'll be there in about a half hour, if I can catch the next bus." She hung up on him before he had a chance to say more.

Shelley told Wayne and Francesca they could tell anyone who called that she was going home early. If headquarters didn't like it, tough. She finally had her priorities in order.

As soon as she walked through the front door of her apartment, Ross seized her in a crushing embrace. "Let's be furious in a moment," he muttered. "Right now, I just need you to hold me."

He kissed her with hot longing, with rough passion, with unending need. A man of great needs, she thought fleetingly, before desire engulfed her. It would always be like this between them, she thought. He could deny it all he wanted, but he needed her. On a roll, feeling everything was possible for her today, she pulled her mouth away from his and said, "I love you."

"Je t'aime," he answered, lowering his head to kiss her again.

"What?" she said in a high-pitched voice.

"I love you," he repeated, kissing her neck while she squirmed in his arms. "Stop squirming."

"Ross . . . I . . ." She was totally beside herself. Only one thought came to mind, and it probably wasn't the most appropriate one. "Yesterday afternoon I signed a contract with Keene International,"

"You what?" He looked absolutely shocked.

"I knew they wanted to sign with you, and I couldn't let you ruin my career like that, but then I talked to Francesca, and she made me realize, though she maybe didn't know it, that what I really wanted was to be as good as you. Not because I really wanted to be as good as you so much, but because I wanted you to respect me so you could love me, which I guess you do anyhow, and I see it was silly now, but I still feel that it's important, and, oh, Ross, you wouldn't believe the things — Mmm-mmm —"

Her words were stifled by the pressure of his hand over her mouth. "Have you lost your mind?" Shelley shook her head. Then she shrugged. "Let me get this straight. You found out I'd clinched Keene's contract on Monday, so you went there and actually got them to sign a contract with you?"

"That's right. And I know you're probably furious, but if you'll just consider —"

"Oh, Shelley, Shelley," he sighed. "You've ruined everything."

"I have?" she asked in a small voice.

"Well, 'ruined' is a little strong," he admitted. "But you've certainly postponed everything. No wonder Elite brought me here! We turn our backs for four days, and you muck up the works."

She bristled. "If you can forget your professional problems for a moment, I want to talk about us."

"I *am* talking about us!" He made a visible effort to calm himself. "Oh, Shelley, why do you think I was in such a rush to finalize that deal? So I could get out of here and take you with me. This situation is impossible for us. We can't keep sleeping together every night and working against each other every day. I'm in love with you, and that's just not good enough anymore."

"Funny, that's what I was going to say."

"Good, at least we're on the right track. You were so certain that, if I got that contract, you'd lose your job. Since you're too unreasonable to quit, I figured the only way to free you was to get you fired."

"You actually had the nerve, the utter unmitigated gall — Where were you going to take me?" she asked, forgetting her outrage at his presumptuousness for a moment.

"That's what we have to discuss. That's where I've been all week. I was sure they'd have requested your resignation by now."

"They're promoting me."

"Oh, great! This is all we need!"

She threw her arms up in exasperation. "Can't you be supportive for even a minute? A woman's lover isn't supposed to be sorry she wasn't fired!"

"And what are they promoting you to? Where are they sending you?"

"California," she informed him angrily.

"California? And how do you expect *me* to feel about that?"

"You needn't get so hostile. I'm not going!"

"What do you mean you're not going?"

"I'm quitting!" She enjoyed the reaction she got to that.

"You're quitting?"

"Yes. Ross, you couldn't look more astonished if I told you I was a Soviet agent."

He stumbled over to the couch and fell onto it without his usual grace. He lay back and flung an arm over his eyes. "I can't believe this. I can't believe it. I've done everything I could to get you to quit. When it was obvious, beyond the shadow of a doubt that you wouldn't, I actually looked forward to seeing you get fired, because I thought it was the only way we could get married. You were so uptight about your commitment to them —"

"Get married?"

He was practically mumbling to himself now. "It seemed the only way. I'd put Elite on top with one bold move and resign. You'd get fired. Off we'd go, happily ever after." He glared at her. "I had thought of everything. Now, thanks to you, I'll be here for months working on a new strategy, since I promised Henri I wouldn't leave him in the lurch. And you will be in California. Unless you quit, which is what I've been asking you to do all along. How can I keep up with this inconsistency? How can you be so unreasonable?" he demanded.

She jumped on top of him. "Slow down! Wait a minute!"

"You're a fine one to say that," he said irritably. "Four days in France, *four days,* and you manage to ruin everything."

"You were in Paris telling Henri you're going to resign because of me? So we could get married?"

"That was yesterday. The rest of the time I was checking out a language school that's for sale in Nice."

"Why?"

"Because it looked like the best prospect of all the ones that are for sale right now, and it's got the advantage of being near the house I own. Of course, thanks to you, we can't go there for months now —"

"Don't you think you should have asked me first, Ross, before you got me fired, married me, and transported me to work in France and live in your house there?"

"Of course I do. That's why I asked you to come home to talk to me today. I had a million questions to ask you. Like, will you marry me; do you want to work with me; does a school in Nice sound good to you; would you like to live in my farmhouse there; and if not, what would you like to do that includes me — because nothing, *nothing* is going to keep me from marrying you. Unless you say no. Which, of course, I'll talk you out of."

Shelley sat up and looked at him in silence for a long time, taking it all in. "Well, gosh," she said inanely.

"Thanks for that positive reinforcement, darling," he said dryly.

"When did you plan all this?"

"Sunday, I guess."

"Sunday! You move awfully fast, don't you?"

"So I've been told."

"Well . . . tell me about this school in Nice."

"Will you marry me?"

"Well, yes, I guess I'll have to after all the trouble you've gone to."

"Shelley!" he said in exasperation.

She smiled and threw herself back on top of him. She kissed him long and affectionately, adoring him, loving him. "I love you. Of course I'll marry you. I would love to work with you, especially now that I've beaten you at least once. You'll have to respect me now."

"I've always —"

"I like Nice, and I'm sure your house is beautiful. But I can't agree to going until you tell me more," she said reasonably.

"It's an independent operation, losing money because it's badly managed. It's in a good location, and the competition isn't that over- whelming. I've got the capital we'll need for the first couple of years."

"My mom told me to marry rich," Shelley teased.

"Yeah, and my mom told me to marry a good cook. But then, I never listened to her, anyhow."

"I want to see this school before I agree to anything."

"You'll have to go alone, then. I can't go anywhere till I sort out the mess you've created for me."

"You'll think of something," she said confidently.

He kissed her. "It's no use trying to stay mad at you," he whispered. "Tell me when you can go, and I'll set it up."

"Next month would be good, I guess. I'm going to resign on Monday, and I'll give just two weeks' notice. It's all they deserve. Then, as soon as you wrap things up here, we can get on with our lives."

"Hmm, good." He started kissing her.

"Oh, by the way, Wayne wanted a job with Elite, although now that he's been promoted, too, he may have changed his mind. Francesca wants one, too."

"Definite possibilities for Francesca," Ross said, thinking of the secretary he didn't trust, "but Wayne is just too uncouth. He belongs with an outfit like Babel."

"Hey! I worked for them for two years."

"Ah, but you're a peacock among pigeons."

"Oh. Well, when you put it that way . . ."

"We're going to be unbeatable. And inseparable," he said with satisfaction.

"Sure, but if our kids are as incorrigible as you, we're in for trouble."

He sighed wearily. "Let's just hope they're not. Besides, you'll keep them in line. See what a good job you're doing with me?"

"Are you sure you're really ready to settle down this time?" Shelley asked, nuzzling his neck and unbuttoning his shirt.

"Absolutely. I've figured out what was missing the last time I tried it. You." His hands slid under her blouse, sure and knowing.

Shelley swallowed, feeling passion flood through her. "Oh, Ross, I'm so glad you came to town."

"So am I. Though if I'd known what it would be like sometimes, I might have run the other way in terror when I got here."

"Not you. That would have been the safe way out." She kissed him. "I love you."

"I love you," he breathed against her lips.

"Let's go to bed. It's been five whole days. It's like starving."

"Yes, it is," he agreed. "I'm so hungry for you . . ." He pulled her to her feet and led her into the bedroom.

"Can we get married in Chicago after I resign?" she said as he started undressing her.

"Okay. I'll live here till we leave Cincinnati"

"Okay." She gasped. "Oh, do that again. Mmm . . ."

"Tu sei la piu bella donna in tutto il mondo."

"That's quite a good line," she admitted. "What else did your Italian buddy teach you?"

"Vuoi una cigaretta?"

"I don't smoke." She caught her breath as he unfastened her bra and let it drop to the floor.

"How about *cerco un momento estatico,"* he murmured, his lips hot against her breasts.

She slid his shirt from his shoulders and trailed her hands across his hard chest. "I want more than just one ecstatic moment with you."

"I couldn't agree more," he said as he slid her skirt down her hips. "I love to touch you, Shelley."

"And you do it so well," she whispered, pressing her breasts against his chest. Everything about him excited her.

She started unbuckling his belt, eager to touch every part of him.

"It's like learning a language," he told her. "I get even better with daily practice."

She laughed as he tumbled her onto the bed, murmuring to her in loving English, intimate French, inept Italian and even garbled Arabic. She opened herself to him, body, and soul, giving and taking love, and knew that this special magic would always exist between them, in any language.

About the Author

Laura Leone is the award-winning author of more than a dozen romance novels. Under her real name, Laura Resnick, she is also an award-winning science fiction/fantasy author. You can find her on the Web at www.sff.net/people/laresnick.